Leftovers

Nikki Adkins

Dedication

This book is dedicated to my Ava. I hope you find a way
to heal.

Chapter One: Leftovers

Don't pity the wicked who created their situation. It is Treason to the innocent.

Don't pity me. The only constant I've had in my life is pity. Even upstairs, above the grey carpeted steps, down the narrow hall, through the wooden dingy door, I've heard the whispers. They echo in my room like the last thuds of a dying man's heart. You get used to them and numb to their sound unless they stop. When entering a room, the mutters come to a halt, and all eyes are on me. Some look me in the face with sorrow on their brows and lips contorted. Some are too uncomfortable to divert their eyes from the floor.

It's not her fault. She's had a hard life. Obviously, she's damaged; look what she's been through. She just needs more love and attention. It's not her talking; it's the trauma speaking. She's just SO sensitive. She just needs someone to talk to. You must be careful with her. She's made of glass; if you push her, she will shatter...

They're not wrong. I am damaged. Amber took everything from me from the moment she gave me life. She shackled me. I would have rather been completely discarded, thrown away like trash, then left to endure the repercussions of her poor decisions. She traded my heart for power. She traded my flesh for companionship. She traded my safety for desire. She traded my trust for loyalty. In the end, she'll trade my memories for revenge.

I've been treated like leftovers my whole life by her. But this will be the only time I will admit that out loud. She feasted on the attention I brought her when she brought me into this world, but after the feast was over, so was her desire to mother me. So, into a Tupperware bowl, I went, to be placed into the back of her life and forgotten, rotting from the inside out. Like leftovers, she tried to pawn me off on others. Her fridge was too full to fit both me and whatever flavor of the week she was able to scrape up. One of us had to go, and if it weren't for my father, she might have crammed me into the garbage disposal once and for all.

For a long time, I was led to believe my father never wanted me. I was made to believe that, like her, he also looked me over like leftovers and found a whole new family. He found a new woman to love. He had a new son he could bond with. He had a new baby… a girl he could easily replace me with. I was made to believe I was nothing to him. What she failed to share was

She was the one who was unfaithful.

She was the one confused about who fathered me.

She was the one who chose to live with another man.

She was the one to refuse visitation after the paternity test.

She was the one using me as a pawn to gain power over him.

She withheld me for spite.

She never had as much power as she did when she strung my heart to dry. When she dangled me over him, he was always out of reach. She thrived on him begging to see me, to keep me, even if it could only be for one day, to be able to visit me on a holiday. What little she granted him, she could take away with the tips of her fingers across her phone's text. Excuses after excuses. She even feigned that it was me, a young toddler at best, who was making the decision whether to go or not. She traded my heart, my right to be loved by my own father, to feel powerful. Even though I am old enough to see the truth for what it was, her words still have power over me. She knows just how to slice her words through me.

"He never loved you. He stole you from me to hurt me, not to love you. He will never choose you. He loves his wife more than you. He loves his stepson more than you (and he's not even blood). He loves his new daughter more than you. You are still nothing to him".

She took love from me. She shackled my heart to the cold, dead remnants within her own chest.

I wish love was all that she had taken. Instead, I got to play house with her and her boyfriend. The only problem was when she wasn't home…he still wanted to play, but I had to be the mommy instead. She let him take my innocence. She chose him even after I confessed what kinds of games I played with him. Even after their separation, she was *kind* enough to continue sending me to him for sleepovers at his new place with his new girlfriend and new kids. I learned to fear bedtime. As I lay on the top bunk with my new *friends,* clutching my eyes closed, pretending to sleep, they took turns caressing my skin with their own toddler-sized fingers. Fingers lurking in dark places they didn't belong, touching me the same ways he used to enjoy. Willing to get through this night. Eyes squeezed shut, hidden by the dark shadows of the room, I let silent tears fall from my eyes.

She traded my flesh to a monster so she wouldn't have to be alone. She slept like a baby while I SCREAMED out from my bed…night terrors and sweats…at four years old. She never asked what my nightmares entailed because, selfishly, she already knew. She failed to protect me from the prying eyes of the devil himself, from the blistering touch that still leaves my skin on fire and holes in my heart. She shackled my dreams of being a child to her lonely soul.

It wasn't long before her desire to be wanted reared its ugly head again. Such a short-lived reprieve where I thought, for once, she may start to love me again. She may have learned to have the instinct that all other mothers seem to have to protect me. Those were wasted wishes on a candle.

Luckily, her next boyfriend didn't like to play house with me. He didn't like me at all. Hell, to be honest, he didn't like her. They knew each other through her last boyfriend. They were cousins. This one was full of rage. He wasn't afraid to slap her around, peering eyes from behind the furniture or not. With the amount of hate that steamed off him, it was surprising that they conceived a child at all. After belittling both of us, beating her and throwing things at me, you'd think she would have had enough. But no. After clinking the blade of a knife against the edge of the crate, threatening to slit the poor dog's throat in front of me simply for barking, this still wasn't enough to make her leave.

Even after eventually bringing my mother to her knees in the yard with the cold barrel of a pistol to her head, she still chose him. By miracle alone, he let her up. She stammered into the house, fresh grass stains on her skin, and went inside to make his dinner. If it weren't for the neighbors, there is a good chance all three of us, my mother, me, and my new sister, would be dead by now. She visited him in jail (ironic, considering she never visits me). She was sorry that she made him hit her. She was sorry he had one felony already, and being caught with an illegal firearm made things worse. She was sorry she angered him so much he wanted to kill her. The only thing she was not sorry for was the trauma she caused me.

It was my fault for always being so whiny. It was my fault I was spying on them as he struck her. I was in the way when he threw that controller. If I could just learn to be invisible, I wouldn't have always caused him to be so angry. If I had just been playing out back like she said, I wouldn't have witnessed her on her knees begging for her life with makeup smeared down her face. It's my fault she can't be with him anymore.

She traded my sense of safety for her selfish desire to be wanted and needed by a man. She failed to protect me from the horrors of violence that shook my childhood. She shackled my spirit to her bruised body.

As a saving grace, the court placed a no contact order between them. My mother cried for a month straight. Slowly, she pulled herself from that quicksand of a relationship and started acting like a mother again. I was blessed with a stretch of calm. She was going to be better. She was going to love me. She was going to finally let go of her abuser. My Grandma Amanda would help her and take care of us so she could get onto her own feet. Turns out, there is a calm before a storm. Another storm of desperation. She let this storm blow her away…to another town…to another home…a home without a refrigerator because she couldn't even be bothered to bring her leftovers.

She abandoned me.

Leftovers

She left me to pull my pieces back together, shattered when she left, with my grandmother so she could start again. To make the wound deeper, she took my sister with her. Not me. Why wasn't I enough for her? How could she love my sister when she couldn't stand to love me? Why wasn't I worthy of love? Why was I such a Goddamn disappointment for her?

She wouldn't take the doe-eyed 7-year-old me. And she wouldn't visit. The only time she called me was when she needed to remind me to lie to my father during his visitation.

Remember to lie when he asks if I came to see you. Remember to tell him I was there with you this week. Remember to tell him that everything is so wonderful with me. And never forget to tell him how much you love me more than you will ever love him.

She traded my trust for loyalty to a man who, in the end, left her the way she left me, just not nearly as broken.

I sheepishly chose to ignore her requests. I knew something big was coming because I heard the salty words exchanged between Amber and my Grandma Amanda. I felt hope that, maybe, for the first time, things could be better. After I met with a gentle woman with a soft-featured face in a very fancy black robe, I shared my secrets. I shared my fears and my sadness. That was the first time I met my lifelong companion: Pity. The tears in her eyes were shed for me. The judge took no mercy on her.

*"She is going to have a hard time adjusting. She likely suffers from PTSD. This is one of the worst cases of mental abuse and manipulation in a child I have ever seen. **Full** legal and physical custody granted to the father".*

My knight in shining armor came for me. He whisked me away to a place where the only touches you felt at bedtime were hugs and snuggles as they tucked me in tight for the night, with wishes that the "bedbugs wouldn't bite." He whisked me away to a place where the only screaming was from excitement (or my new brother Zack playing video games from just one room away). He whisked me away to where the games we played didn't have to be a secret. We played out in the yard, where nobody was forced to get on their knees and beg to live. We played with the dogs that could bark as loud as they wanted and didn't have to fear being strung up by their guts or their throats being splayed open for their vocal cords to be dangled out. We played on the trampoline…and on the swing set…and with the basketball hoop…and with the new bikes and scooters…and in the sprinklers. We played with buckets of dolls, plastic food, and books. We got to play at his mommy's house and my new Grandma Judith, and when it was time to go, we all got to go home, including me. I didn't have to stay behind!

We played dress up with gowns, and my new mommy, Cara, brushed my hair out of my face. She pulled it into ponytails and braids and funny little buns. He whisked me away to where my new little sister, Ella, looked up to me. He whisked me away to where I could act brave or sleep with a nightlight, my choice. He whisked me away to a place where nothing was my fault, and everyone was so proud of me. A place where I felt wanted.

A place where she made me *hate* him for taking me to. A place where she wasn't welcome. She wasn't in control, and she wasn't desirable. SHE was nobody here. She shackled my candor to her filthy, deceitful lips. I was her little ventriloquist doll.

"Enjoy me while you can. I won't be here long. You only got custody because you are a liar. You only got custody because you had a lawyer. You don't love me. You only wanted custody, so you didn't have to pay child support. I don't want to live with you. I hate you. I hate your wife; I will never call her mom. I hate my brother. I hate my new sister. If you loved me at all, you wouldn't have stolen me from her".

Every other weekend, my impressionable mind and childhood memories were constantly recycled with new stories. Stories about wolves and sheep. I was the sheep. Everyone at my new home was wolves dressed impressively like sheep. They didn't love me. They didn't want what was best for me. They were pretending, waiting for me to put my guard down so they could attack. The only way to save myself was to put up walls. She promised me things she knew I longed to hear. "I'm going to get you back. I'm going to let you live with me and your sister. We are going to have our own little family. I'm not going to leave you this time, sis".

She was good at telling stories. I was not. When I told stories about the new zoos, fairs, and camps I got to go to, she couldn't have cared less. She was disgusted when I told stories about the new things I learned to do, like riding a bike, swiveling on a hoverboard, or rowing my very own Kayak. "You must really like your new mommy, huh? She's just so great, isn't she? You don't even love me anymore, do you"? She took her from me. She took the joy I felt and replaced it with memories of guilt. She convinced me my new mom was the worst wolf of them all. The leader of the wolf pack. She implanted stories of hate and maleficence.

She didn't love me. She tolerated me at best. She would never love me like her own. She wants me to be weaker, uglier, dumber, and unloved. My new mom was not to be trusted. Most importantly, never give her the satisfaction of calling her mom. She will never be my mom.

From that day forward, I called her Cara. The guilt of betraying my own mother to love my new mother was more weight than I could carry. When I am all alone now, I wish I had been born with shoulders of steel. Instead, I filled the wall I needed to build with mortar made from sorrow. She traded my happiness for greed.

She didn't want me to show love to anyone else, even if she could never love me in return.

She always treated me like leftovers. But as I said before, don't have pity on me. I just wanted to help you understand why others did and why there were constant whispers. Why did everyone around me feel like they must walk on eggshells? When I first started noticing the pity, I was sad and felt like I deserved it. I was broken.

This made me feel something different, something unexplainable. The more others felt pity, the more they lavished on me. I learned to use it to my advantage. I earned leniency, gifts, and special attention. I could influence others that pitied me, giving me more power. I wasn't going to be leftovers anymore.

Something bad, but oddly familiar, was sparking within me. I intentionally sabotaged relationships. I hurt people who couldn't fight back. I fed off the guilt of others. Without knowing it, I had let her consume me…and there wouldn't be any leftovers. Just a bad taste in everyone's mouth that got in my way. Here's the part where you learn that I wasn't only shackled to her. I was unapologetically becoming her.

Chapter Two: Meet Ava

I'm not a child anymore. If this were a Disney movie, I would be old enough to be kissed awake by a prince and married, riding off into the sunset. But I'm not living in a fairytale. Junior year has started. I'm so close to being an adult, but I am more confused than ever. Not just about what my next steps after high school are, but with everything I thought I knew. I have been a complete menace for the last two years. I have been making poor choices left and right. I have told so many stories I literally struggle with remembering which ones are true and which ones I fabricated myself.

If I am going to tell this story, I guess I better start by telling some facts upfront. My name is Ava. I just reached my sweet 16th birthday. I still live with Liam, Cara, and Ella. Zack moved out. Went up to college. Sometimes, I wish I could just get away. But the only person you can't run from is yourself.

We live in a cookie-cutter house in suburbia. One of the nicest homes in the cul-de-sac. Everyone in the neighborhood is friendly. You know the type. Everyone waves at everyone and chats each other up in the street when they walk their dogs and check their mail. I used to love this neighborhood. That was until my best friend broke up with me one year ago. Don't worry; that story is for another time. I'm just beginning.

The high school is nice. The new principal is not. For the last two years, students have been running this school. Rules to the wind. Most students ditched class. Girls gathered in the bathroom stalls, sharing vapes during class. Others tell nasty rumors about the same girls they sat with every day at the lunch table. Girls gather around the mirror, puckering their lips, hunching their backs, and taking pictures of themselves. Some of us peeled off our sweatshirts, revealing tiny shirts, barely long enough to cover our pushup bras, rolling up our shorts to make the 2.5-inch inseam even shorter. Ass cheeks peeking out from the denim. We all wanted to dress this way. Only later, roll your eyes and wrinkle your nose when you see another girl dressed the same. *Slut.*

Those were the good ol' days before this principal came through and started demanding the faculty do their job and enforce the policies. It feels like a tragedy to leave a $1200 phone in my locker when I could be surfing it instead of listening to a teacher drone on and on about unimportant things like life skills and math. He has the teachers actually taking attendance and calling parents when we don't show up to class. Monitors with live feeds line the hallways. I swear he must have been a warden in another life.

Right before school let out for the summer last year, I started dating Mitchell. He's been pretty good to me. He has a job already. He doesn't mind buying me things. Sometimes, I feel bad for the way I manipulate him. He's had a girlfriend before me, but not many. He's very impressionable, but that's one of the things I like about him best. I can talk him into whatever I want. I mean, we've only been dating for four months, and I already made him buy me a promise ring. Shit, I talked him into getting a tattoo of my name on his collarbone out of somebody's garage. The kid's an idiot.

He believes everything I say, though. I love it. He thinks he's going to save me from a tower or something. I've sat up countless nights filling his head with horror stories. I'm basically Cinderella in the stories I tell him. He can't believe it. He feels so bad for me. The pity just drips and pools off his lips when he talks to me. Sometimes, I worry one of my old friends will tell him the truth. At this point, even if the truth slapped him in the face, I'm not sure he would believe it. I have him wound so tightly around my finger that it's pathetic.

Mitchell was easy to convince. There aren't many people who will still go along with my stories. The problem with telling lies is that you must have a good memory. You must remember who you told what lie to and what exactly the lie entailed. Honestly, I used to have many more people wrapped around my fingers than I actually had fingers. I got greedy. I was getting fat with all the attention I was eating up. My stories started getting too elaborate. I couldn't help myself. People started questioning me, challenging my stories. Things weren't adding up. I got sloppy, and I lost some followers along the way. Other than Mitchell, my mother and Grandma Judith are the only two people I am still stringing along. Judith would follow my stories through a dark cave and over a cliff, even if she literally saw the drop-off coming.

On the other hand, my mother knows I am lying, but this is the first time she is listening to me, engaged and animated in the things I say, so I keep it up. Instead of leftovers, she's treating me like dessert. She can't get enough.

Truth be told, I got myself into a pickle, which isn't super surprising nowadays. I got caught up feeding her so many lies that I'm pretty sure there is no backtracking now. There is no safety net for when this all falls through. I have convinced her that everything is terrible at my father's. I am being all but beaten here. I have made them out to be the very wolves she warned me of. These are the only stories she has ears for. When I start a story about how awful things are for me, she literally finishes my story with an ending she has created herself. It's like a twisted book we are writing together. I should feel ashamed, but for now, I have her attention.

Jealousy is complicated. Sometimes, I think she hates my father for moving on. Sometimes, I think she hates him because he was the best guy she has ever had, and she took him for granted. Other times, I think she hates him because she can't have him. No matter what advances she tries and crude comments she makes towards him, "I hear you're moving. I have a box you can use", he doesn't give her the time of day. Then again, maybe she despises him because he did something with his life. He isn't somebody who peaked in high school and never made it out of the trailer park like her. When I am really hopeful, I think it could be because he took me from her, and it broke her heart, and it's never really healed since that day nine years ago.

Loathing. That's what she has always felt for Cara. Cara's presence has been like a virus to Amber. The first glimpse of Cara's beauty and perkiness seeped through the thin corneal membrane of Amber's eyes sixteen years ago when they first met and spread disdain through each vessel of her body. Amber was a curious cat, requesting to meet the woman who would be caring for her baby overnight when Liam came to get me at just months old. Curiosity killed her. Cara was independent, working, going to school, and already a mother herself. She was friendly and confident. She showed no apprehension in caring for an infant and, more so, seemed pleased to do it. Not to mention the way she looked at Liam; smitten.

Almost two years ago, Amber waltzed back into my life. She explained that she had made a mistake and was ready to be a mother to me again. She never apologized to me for any single thing that she allowed to happen to me in the past. In fact, she explained to me that she was the victim. My father was always working and didn't have time to be with her at home all day. He would even come home

5-10 minutes late sometimes, so she knew he was cheating on her, probably with someone from work. He would lie and say he would hang out with his dad, but she knew he was really hanging out with some other girl. His dad would even answer his phone and lie to her. That's why she had to find another boyfriend. She was just so lonely.

When she found out she was pregnant, my father had already moved home with his dad. She was living with her new boyfriend, so good riddance…well, until she had me and realized I was Liam's. He went ahead and took the paternity test, but you know, he never actually wanted me. He probably wanted her to have an abortion. He was probably hoping it would say he wasn't the father. He barely even helped her with me. The $500 he was giving her a month in child support was barely enough (oh wait, I always forget the part where he was never even paying the child support). She was hardly scraping by between her EBT installments, WIC, Medicaid, and Section 8 housing. I mean, that's why she had to keep all the clothes he bought for me at her house because she could barely afford to buy me anything new. That's why she couldn't spare any diapers, wipes, or formula, and he would have to buy all new supplies every time he picked me up. That's why she had to send me to his house in plastic play shoes and wait for him to buy new ones for her to keep at her house.

She filled me in that she was very secretively trying to get more visitation with me, but would you believe that prick would never let her have any additional time with me? That's why she never came down to see me on the Wednesdays the court order allowed. He made her feel like it would be a burden for her to come see me. That's why she could never come to see me, not even once a month. He just made her feel so uncomfortable. That's why even when she was scheduled to get me for my birthday, she didn't bother. He would just try to "one up" any gift she got me. You know, he was buying my love and affection. When she lost custody and lost her $500 paycheck, it was just too hard for her to drive the hour to see me or come watch me at any of my games. He shouldn't have been so greedy with his money. If he had paid her more, then she could have saved up for a car. How was she supposed to work over the years? She had 3 other children and no fathers for any of them. She was a single mother.

She was a victim too. It wasn't just me that endured violence. She has anxiety and panic attacks. It's not her fault that she wasn't able to take care of me. She didn't know that just because a guy had a criminal record and had been incarcerated for violence, he would be a bad choice. She's on medication now. Sometimes, when she takes a few more of the Xanax than prescribed, she must sleep it off for the entire day, but how else is she supposed to heal? My father looks down on her for being "mentally unstable". He's not perfect though. She explained to me that I should have way more freedom than I do. He's too strict. And Cara, Cara shouldn't have a say at all.

She's not even my mother. I don't have to listen to her. They shouldn't be making decisions for me. I am almost an adult. Why should I have to follow their rules? Why should I have to help around their house? I didn't ask to be there.

If I tell the judge I want to live with her now, I can do whatever I want. No more chores, no more homework, no more bedtimes, no more restrictions on anything. I don't even have to finish high school if I don't want to. She educated me. You don't even have to have a baby to collect Welfare. Then, I wouldn't even have to work if I didn't want to. If I come to live with her, my father will have to start paying her child support again, and she promises that she will just give me the money every month so I won't even have to work. My boyfriend isn't allowed to stay the night at my father's house with me, but if I come to live with her, he can stay all weekend if he wants to. There is nothing my father can give me that she can't.

The stipulation…all I must do is convince everyone that I have always hated living with him. He is verbally and mentally abusive. Cara is a terrible person. She has always treated me poorly. She has always cut me down and treated me like I was beneath everyone else. I just have to tell people that I have never been able to be my true self in his house. I am so uncomfortable and have never felt loved. I just have to start acting out. If I am bad enough, he will just give me back to her. She doesn't quite have the money for a lawyer, so this will be the best way.

Don't look a gift horse in the mouth, right? This is what I have wanted since I was seven years old. I just wanted her to choose me for once. It may have taken her a little while… or nine years, but she is. She is finally choosing me. She wants me to come back home. She is going to make up for all the missed years.

Before you think I am crazy or naïve, let me assure you I know she is lying now, but a child's mind is very impressionable. You can manipulate a child to believe anything you want. Usually, good parents do it to give joy to children. Tricking them into believing in magical things like Santa, the Easter Bunny, and the Tooth Fairy. I won't tell you what kind of parent Amber is.

Nevertheless, I want to believe her so badly. I want to forget the stories I am about to tell you. I want to pretend there isn't a pattern to her madness. I want to believe that she just genuinely wants to establish a relationship and simply love me. Did you feel that? It was pity. You feel it, and I have barely even begun.

Chapter Three: No Pity for the Privileged

8 years old: Pity truly only leaves us silenced and ashamed.

Liam never broke his promises. He showered me with gifts. New clothes, shoes, and toys. I didn't have my very own room yet. I shared it with my little sister, but it was nice not to be alone at night. The boogie man comes out at night. The night scares me.

The only thing that scares me about this room is that Ella has a "my size doll." It only stands 3 feet tall but might as well be 6 feet tall, the way, it creeps me out. It has long, straight, dusky brown hair. Its dark brown eyes follow me around the room. There is always a hint of a smirk on its face. It doesn't have "baby" clothes on. The doll wears a long-sleeved white shirt with a jean vest. It has its own little jean pants and boots.

She has had the doll for a long time. When I used to come down to visit on the weekends, Cara would have Liam put the doll away in the hallway cupboard, top shelf, so that I didn't have to worry about the doll *getting me*. The worst part about the doll is that Ella named it Lilly D. She used to watch a show called "The Haunting Hour" by R.L. Stine. She named it after a doll that slowly comes alive to take over the body of the little girl that owns her. Fitting. I don't like that doll at all, and I worry it will try to take me over. The doll turns up all over the house. Ella swears she didn't move it.

Ella loves the doll, but she gets rid of her for me. Ella beats the doll up to make sure she can't just climb out of the trash can and sneak into the house when someone lets the dog out. She removes her limbs, and we have dad put her in a trash bag and take her out to the can on the curb for the trashmen the next morning to pick up. Ella is a great sister for giving her doll up for me. I will do my best to be her new best friend so she doesn't have to miss her doll.

For the first time, I did have my very own bed. It was a real bed you couldn't just fold up and put away during the day when company came over. I got to pick out my very own sheets and blankets. They didn't even have cigarette holes burned into them. I didn't have to share any of my things. He got me my very own little desk and matching chair. He got me a little nightlight and a "baby" monitor, even though I wasn't a baby anymore. I didn't have to be scared and alone for too long. He could hear me fussing and rustling in my sleep and could rush in to comfort me after I awoke startled from my sleep, drenched in sweat and despair, from the terrors that still haunted me at night.

He got me enrolled in a school that wasn't too far away. He or Cara was able to drive me to and from school. My Grandma Amanda didn't have a car, so I used to ride a small shuttle to school.

It was always filled with strangers, and I used to squish down in my seat, hoping not to draw attention to myself. I was a shy little girl going into the third grade. The teacher was wonderful, and I could tell that she could see I was a smart little girl even though I didn't like to speak up in class. Embarrassed about what others were thinking about me. I found friends that didn't know to pity me. I could be a new me, not just a broken little girl.

When I was still in my ventriloquist phase, my father took me to see yet another kind woman in a small little room. She let me talk about whatever I wanted and never pushed me to talk about the things I didn't. She said, "This is a safe place, and you can tell me anything you want to, and I won't tell anyone else". I met with a counselor once weekly to help me adjust to my new home. Sometimes, he and Cara would also attend the sessions. The counselor said it would be best to have consistent expectations and boundaries for a child who came from such a disruptive environment. While I sat at a small table, putting the pieces of the wooden puzzle together, I could hear her whispers. "Children like Ava are not used to a stable environment. They are always awaiting the chaos to erupt. She needs love, patience, and understanding while she adjusts to her new home. She's not used to not getting all the attention all at once. She won't want to share that with her siblings. If she desires attention, she will get it either positively or negatively. When she displays negative behaviors to get attention,

IGNORE it. When she realizes she can't get attention in that manner, the behavior should dissipate".

She wanted to take the pity away. She wanted me to be treated like a "normal" girl. Up until that moment, that is what I thought I wanted as well. Something inside my mind whispered my mother's words. "You aren't going to be special anymore. And if you're not special, then you won't be worthy of his love". And that scared me more.

My brother Zack played soccer. My father and Cara would haul us to the soccer field to watch him play. All eyes were on him as he dashed up and down the field in his oversized striped shirt and tall matching socks. The smile smeared on their faces made me sad. I wanted to be him. I needed their eyes to be on me. I wanted to impress them and have them tell everyone how great I was. Cara was happy to comply. She signed all three of us up the following season. I loved that cotton jersey. It was my time to shine. I could just imagine her telling my father just how proud she was of me, how hard I kicked that ball, how fast I could hustle up and down the field. And she did. She took pictures and selfies with just the two of us. She didn't want to live this moment with me once. She wanted to remember our time together forever. That made me beam with delight.

The only problem was she did the same thing for Ella. Her

eyes filled with enthusiasm for her. She laughed lightly watching the young girls on her team rushing around chasing the ball, bumping into one another. *She will never love you the way she loves her.* What's worse is my father would also come to our games when work permitted it. He followed suit and complimented both of us. But I always felt like I could hear just a smidge bit more joy and pride when he spoke about Ella. I hated her for making me share his love with her. At his house, I wasn't supposed to have to share anything…well, except that room. If he was proud of her, he couldn't possibly be proud of me. I reeked with jealousy. How could she be so naïve to think she wasn't causing me to lose his love? Why did she have to copy everything I did?

During her games, I would try to make a scene. I would try to steal his attention away by telling him stories and showing him cartwheels and summersaults. He would glance my way, smile, nod, and speak words of approval, but it was not enough. His eyes always veered back to her. If telling him how great I could be wasn't working, I would have to conjure up his pity. Lips into a snout facing downward, fists balled by my sides, I marched away from him. I glanced back, hoping to see him chasing after me. I stomped my way over to the other set of bleachers and plopped down, letting out a gruff sigh. With my mind, I commanded him to leave her field side to come pity me. And he did.

However, he and Cara became wise to my efforts. Defeat

fleeted in just as easily as pity had settled. The tables had yet again been turned. Just as that mousey little counselor had advised, when I repeated these efforts to steal the show the next game, he let me sit there alone, sulking. I started to detest soccer. It didn't make me Zack. It couldn't even make me Ella. My coach had his favorite girls as well. Yelling encouragement to my teammates on the field while I stood on the side lines. I wasn't his star player. I never even scored a single goal. There would be no celebration for just me at the end of the game.

I asked my mother just once if maybe she could come down to watch me play. She scowled at the idea. It was too far away; you know, an entire one hour away. She couldn't be bothered to get off the couch to come see me. She didn't have any excuses. She didn't work. My little sister was getting big enough that she could bring her along. There was no reason at all. The thing about her was she never felt like I deserved a reason. Needing to plead with her should have been a sign that she would never choose me. Hurt drove me to never play soccer again.

The hurt she made me feel wasn't contagious, but I wanted to spread it. I thought maybe it was like dirt on your hands. If you touched other things, they got a little dirty, but your hands got a little cleaner. I thought if I let some of my hurt out, I wouldn't feel it so deeply inside. I wanted to make Ella hurt just a little bit. After all, she inadvertently hurt me when she got the attention I wanted. I would take some of her favorite Monster High dolls and rip off their heads. She would be upset when she found them. Cara would superglue their heads back onto their necks. It was only a minor inconvenience. I secretly let out some of my hurt, and Cara pulled out the superglue.

This newfound scrutiny of other people's intentions leaked into other aspects of my life. I became close to one girl at my new school, Dakota. She was nice and I could tell that her home life was also not rainbows and sunshine, but she still had a smile on her face to greet me with every day. She also lived with her father full-time, and it seems that her mother also abandoned her. We didn't give each other pity, just conversation. She had a little sister as well. Luck, falling the way it has been in my mind lately, would have it that her little sister was the same age as my little sister. At first, I liked the idea that both of us could go down there and have a friend to play with. We would all play together, and it was nice until it wasn't. I started having those same intrusive thoughts that maybe my friend Dakota would learn to like my little sister better than she liked me. Maybe she would leave me like leftovers as well. Jealousy curdled in the depths of my stomach.

Unbeknownst to Dakota, I started having sour thoughts about our friendship. While I would lay awake at night, the thoughts would play on repeat in my mind. These thoughts transformed into snide comments and head nods of agreement when other girls at school started calling her weird and gross. I didn't want to be associated with her anymore. That would mean I was also weird and gross. That was not the reputation I wanted at school. I wanted to start new. At my last school, I had a friend who kept giving me head lice. I always hoped that I wouldn't have been known as "the headlice kid". Cara would spend back-breaking hours hunched over the couch, picking every little bug and nit out of my hair when I came back from my mom's visit. Just when she would get my hair clean, bam, another visit and another fresh batch of headlice infested the tangles of my hair and scrolled along my scalp.

When the time was right, I took the opportunity to tell those pretty-faced girls not to hang out with Dakota because she had head lice (which was true). Cara used to make me wear my hair in braids around her when we played, and she would dribble tea tree oil in my hair to deter any bugs that thought about staying. They erupted in laughter. They pretended to shed themselves of invisible bugs and scratched at their scalps. They took my hand, and we ran around the playground that day. In that half hour, I felt untouchable and wanted. The self-pity and corrupted thoughts I created in my own mind paid out in a way that made me feel worthy of their friendship. I let Dakota down. Unsurprisingly, she didn't want to speak to me after that day. I simmered for a moment in sadness for a friendship lost. I just sped up the inevitable. She was going to leave me anyway; it was just a matter of time.

However, the unthinkable happened. That wondrous half hour I spent galloping around the playground just the afternoon before was gone. I was not invited to gallop around today. I was not invited to sit with them during lunch. I was not privy to the secrets and giggles they shared. I was alone. My biggest fear manifested. I took scraps of food from my Styrofoam tray and snuck into the bathroom. I ate in solidarity, hidden behind the walls of the bathroom stall for a couple of weeks. I felt shame for what I had done, but I would not apologize for my misdoings.

Dangerously, I began to start pitying myself. I was outcasted away, sitting on that ceramic stool, casting daggers at my reflection through the crack of the stall.

If it weren't for Cara signing me up to play that stupid game. If it weren't for Ella stealing all my attention. If it weren't for Dakota laughing and smiling Ella's way while we played. If it weren't for friendship circles that I could never be a part of.

I festered in my pity for myself. Didn't they know I was damaged? Didn't they know I needed more love and more attention than everyone else? Didn't they care at all?

Chapter Four: Stain and Spoil

9 years old

Zack is perfect. He's three years older than me, in middle school already. He's tall, skinny, smart, funny, and charismatic. Everyone just loves him. He doesn't have a problem making and keeping friends like me. Ella just loves his attention. She used to follow me around, but now she wants to follow HIM around. She wants to sit in his room and watch him play games. My father wants to take him fishing and bike riding. I see that he is the son my father always wanted. He probably never wanted a daughter. When Zack speaks, everyone listens. When Zack tells a joke, everyone laughs. Cara is absolutely mesmerized by him. Everyone else is fooled by him, but not me. I know he has flaws.

For one, I know he's not really that great. He also has a dad who doesn't want anything to do with him. He hadn't seen his own father in almost ten years. His father doesn't call him or, visit him or beg to see him on the weekends. How great of a kid could he be if his own father didn't want to see him?

He's lazy. He must be told repeatedly to clean up his room. He's constantly reminded to stop growing mold in the dishes under his bed. He has chores assigned to him but never gets them done without someone badgering him. Everything is disorganized and thrown amuck in his room. He hardly showers. Cara constantly interrogates him. "When was the last time you showered? Oh, you're not sure. Right. That means it's been too long". She demands that he do it that day.

He's spoiled. Everything he asks for, he gets. Just because he's a boy, he doesn't have to share a room with anyone else. We're not supposed to go into his room or play with any of his things. There's only one person that doesn't spoil him. That makes me thankful for her. Sometimes, I'm pretty sure Grandma Judith forgets he exists. She brings over treats and gifts and often forgets to bring him something. On Easter, she brought me and Ella big stuffed animals and baskets. She brought him nothing. I like that Grandma Judith doesn't treat him like he's perfect. She doesn't acknowledge or ask him to stay at her house like she does us.

I don't like how Cara will speak out to Grandma Judith for doing these things (or not doing them). I don't like that Cara stands up for him. It hurts me that he isn't a disappointment to her. Even though his dad doesn't want to see him, she puts so much effort into making him feel special and loved. She showers him with affection even though it's clear he doesn't always want it. She doesn't become irate even when he tells her that he didn't meet her expectations. She would never let my father throw things at him when he was angry. I secretly wish she didn't love him. I am envious of what he takes for granted. I want to treat him like a carpet and trample all over him. I want to stain him.

Snitching is the easiest way to help him fall from his perch on the pedestal. I've heard him swear a few times in the night when talking to his friends, and I don't tell Cara; I tell my father. I tell on him for staying up later than bedtime. I tell about him eating the last of the crackers and leaving the box in the cupboard. I tell on him for not doing his chores. Where I can sense annoyance from my father, Zack still seems unbothered.

I know my father cannot stand whining. So, I started sneaking around "borrowing" Zack's things without asking. I start "accidentally" breaking his Legos. I snicker from my room, hearing Liam yelling at him for always snitching on his sister. I know I won't see any consequences from these actions. My mother has become more distant, and that will create pity for me. Where pity lives, so does leniency. A good person would stop there, but the lines become more blurred for me every day. When dad and Cara turn out the lights for the night, I sneak across the hall and open Zack's backpack. I slowly remove sheets of homework from his bag and then glide the teeth of the zipper back into a sealed position. As his grades slip from missing homework, so does Cara's patience for her perfect little boy.

Just to push him over the edge, I learn to stay awake for as long as he falls asleep. He is a hard sleeper, mouth open with drool gathered in the slits of his lips. I reach over his body and tap the buttons on his alarm, moving it from AM to PM. This part actually frightens me because he doesn't always sleep with his eyes fully shut. Sometimes, they are open, just a slit, but enough that it makes me think any second, he may startle awake and catch me in the act.

He swears he set his alarm. He doesn't know why it didn't go off. He missed the bus multiple days this month. The mystery of his alarm. Cara and dad are getting fed up with him being so irresponsible. *I never miss my alarm.* Tensions grow between dad and Zack. Energy shifts between Zack and Cara. I left the best for last. Unexpectedly, tensions ignite between dad and Cara. Almost nightly, I can hear the voices becoming harsh and quick as they exchange words. I can hear the exacerbation and exhaustion in her tone.

There is something satisfying in watching the once great things fall to debris beneath your feet. My dad looks at him like spoiled milk, curdling in a cup underneath his bed now. He's no longer perched up high, peering down on my inferiority. I am the expectation now. Everything in his days to follow will be compared to me.

"Why can't you just do your chores like Ava without being reminded? Why can't you just get up on time? She's younger than you, you should be the responsible one. It's not her responsibility to look out for you. Ava would never back talk like you do. Ava would never try to blame others for her problems".

I temporarily pull my figurative claws from his skin. The damage has been done. No need to inflict any other wounds for now.

I may be my father's favorite again, but I still feel remorse and disgust inside. My conscience attempts to eat away at me for what I've done. I'm feeling confused about whether he ever actually did anything wrong to me. Why do I want to hurt him? Why do I want others to feel the hurt I feel? I'm almost sick from rolling these questions over in my mind. I shouldn't have wanted to stamp out his light.

I'm just taking back what he stole from me in the first place. I won't be replaced by my own brother. I did what I had to do to earn my dad back.

Let's sidebar for a minute. While planning my takeover, I was also dabbling in a few other activities. During that year, I was trying to be more relatable. Zack was running cross country, so I would be running as well. Girls on the Run is a wonderful organization. It is a program where young girls meet after school and hang out with each other. They build friendships and spread kindness. I was learning to feel more confident about myself that year. While team building and sharing encouragement with one another, you train to complete a fun run, a 5K, at the end of the season. So basically, they took Girl Scouts, cut out the cookies, and taught you to work up a sweat instead.

Seeing how the girls interacted with their moms and how encouraging the coaches were made me miss having a mother. I didn't want to push Cara away anymore (not that I ever really wanted to in the first place). I started seeking her out. I would wander into her room and pretend to be looking for something; then, I would conveniently sit down on her bed and wait for her to notice me.

She was so easy to talk to. We laughed over fifth-grade drama and who got blasted "accidentally" during Ga Ga Ball at recess. We snorted in laughter about the gross boy who sat in front of me and farted all through English, and the teacher almost had to evacuate the class because of the smell of sewage… and even harder when I revealed sometimes, I was the one who farted and then blamed it on him. She told me crazy tales about her job and the wacky people that came in. She graced me with stories about when I was a toddler and the wonky things I would do. Like, I would be sitting in the backseat, and then I would suddenly screech and freeze in place on repeat.

Bliss. Like falling in love. I felt like she was made to be my mother.

The weather was perfect, cool and sunny. We were in our own little world, jumping and dodging each other on the trampoline. She was bouncing me like an egg, waiting for me to hatch open. Her skin was glistening and the way the sun hit her dark brown hair, it looked like she was wearing a halo. A true guardian angel sent down to heal me. As she sat, breathless, on the black polypropylene net below us, I felt overwhelmingly compelled to blurt it out. "I don't think that my mother loves me. She lies to me. She promises me things and then takes them back". After a painful pause, she looked me dead in the face, pity spilling from her eyes, and told me she believed my mother did love me. She just has a lot going on right now. And that was what I needed at that moment. I loved her for trying to spare me.

As if she were new shoes, I wanted to show her off, flaunt her around, you could say. My friends loved her. My classmates loved her. We were having a class trip to Chicago, and the school was looking for chaperones to come along. I was nervous to ask her. My mother had never come to a single thing I asked. Rejection fleeted through my mind. Unnecessary worry. I hinted around and then went for it, like a cannonball in a pool. It turns out she wasn't about to let me down. We buddied up in the back of the bus. We scoured the Field Museum for answers to my workbook. We scurried down the boardwalk and cycled in the sky on the Ferris wheel. Sleeping soundly into her shoulder on the way home was the perfect ending to a perfect trip.

Chicago went so well that it wasn't even a question that she was the one I wanted to run with me in my upcoming 5K. We could run off into the sunset together. I didn't waste my breath bothering to ask Amber. For once, not a single part of me wanted to, and that felt like what I imagined happiness felt like.

We prepped and jogged. We stretched and danced in the middle of the football field, waiting for the run to start. The coach painted our faces, and I got into my run-day tutu. The track was an easy run, not too hilly. We ran through the woods and jumped over branches and rocks. We passed other parent-kids couples. My dad and Ella stood on the sidelines and cheered us on as we ran past them. Teachers lined the path and high-fived us as we ran past them. It was exhilarating. We were a power team. Everything was perfect…until it wasn't.

As we rounded the last corner of the track and crossed over the finish line, people clapping, us hugging each other, I caught a glimpse of her from the corner of my eye. She was a mirage in the middle of an endless desert. A ghost that had been haunting my dreams, and she was here. She was squished together, shoulder to shoulder, with my Grandma Amanda. Instinctively, I dropped Cara's hand out of mine. I didn't want her to see it. I didn't want her to know. It was like the wound was just about healed, and then she came through and pulled the edges of the scab up just to watch it leak blood all over again.

Apparently, dad knew she might come but didn't want to tell me. He didn't want to get my hopes up because she had a nasty habit of lifting me up just to watch me come plummeting back down. Tell me why her presence there meant more to me than anything Cara had done for me in the entire last year. Actually… don't tell me. I don't want to hear it. She spoils everything.

Chapter Five: Bubble Gum, Palm Trees, and Filth

10 years old

Summer break from school just started, and dad says that we'll be moving. He and Cara have been fixing up the house, planting flowers in all the pots, and growing grass back into the yard, where we ripped it up with the minibike and quad. I feel like I'm going to miss this house. I feel like I'm going to miss swinging on the swing set that I flew so high on that I broke it and fell into the fence. I'm going to miss hiding on the side of the garage and darting along the gate, pretending we were spies and were going to save the day. I'm going to miss playing in the pond out front, catching frogs and praying their pee won't give me warts on my fingers. I'm going to miss the long driveway that I learned to ride my bike and scooter on. I'm even going to miss the basement that always scared me unless somebody else was down there with me. I'm going to miss the laundry chute.

Dad and Cara have found a new house not too far from this house that we are going to move into. It's literally just a few roads away. They say in the new house that we will all have our own bedrooms. I'm excited about this, but also kind of sad. I'm going to miss having Ella in my room to help keep me safe at night. Dad says that we get to choose any color paint we want for our new bedrooms. Well, kind of. Cara told Zack that he could not paint his room black. I'm going to choose the best color. The brightest, most fun color in the whole wide world…. Bubble gum pink. Our room is lavender right now, and I like purple a lot, but pink will be better, brighter, and just plain awesome. It's been decided. Cara is going to spend the whole weekend painting everyone's rooms. I can't wait to see how it turns out.

I went to my mother's trailer this weekend; because it's summer, I would be staying for the week, not just the weekend. I couldn't even wait to tell her about my new house and my new room. She says there was nothing wrong with our old house, and she doesn't know why we would bother moving. She says my dad is turning me into a spoiled brat. She says I don't appreciate anything she has for me. I don't want her to burst my bubble gum bubble of excitement, so I don't tell her about the paint color I chose. I still want to have something happy to think about while I'm here.

As if reading my thoughts, she tells me she has exciting news for me. She tells me she has a surprise for me ready back home at the trailer on our drive home. I wonder what it is, but I don't get my hopes up. When we pull up in the patchy grass next to the trash can and park, I can't help but feel a little spark of excitement. I kind of hope it's a cat. Mom has had 2 dogs now for a few months. I like them, okay, but I would really like a cat. Something to snuggle in my lap and on my pillow at night. She has me close my eyes and walk up to the front door with her. This incites more excitement. When she opens the door, there is no cat purring by my feet. The inside of the trailer looks the same: cluttered. And on the couch sits a strange man. He's chubby and has tattoos on his arms that are faded. He's wearing a plain black Hanes T-shirt and grubby jean shorts. His hair is kind of greasy. When he smiles at me, he has a black tooth in the front. My mother tells me this is my surprise. She wants me to meet her new boyfriend, Kyle.

I don't immediately greet him. She puts her hand on my back and pushes me towards him. My feet stagger across the carpet that matches the grass outside, patchy. My mom gives me another push and tells me not to be rude. I roll my eyes and muster up a hello. She tells me Kyle and her have been officially dating for an entire week now. Since he just got out of jail and doesn't have a job, he's going to be living with us now.

In the kitchen, while she's boiling the water for our Ramen noodles, she tells me Kyle is a really nice guy. She has been talking to him online. She says he is cousins with her first couple of boyfriends. She had met him a few times in person before while she was dating her last boyfriend. She assures me even though he was in jail, it wasn't for violence. He was just in there for breaking into people's homes and stealing. He was going to stay with his mom, but now, because they are in love, he's going to be here.

At least one of us wanted to be here. Looking around, I started to see how dirty her house had become. I finally acknowledged the overwhelming stench of feces. I start to head down the hall to mine and Trudy's room, but my mom yells out that I am not allowed to go in that room anymore. The dogs have been pooping all over the trailer. She says that they mostly pooped in that room, and it's all over the bed and clothes, so I will have to start sleeping on a cot in the living room for now. I wonder for a minute where Trudy is sleeping.

That night while lying on the cot by the front door, I couldn't help but think, *"Why doesn't she just let the dogs go outside to poop"?* My dad lets our dog go outside. We never have poop in the house. Why doesn't she just pick the poop up? If it grosses her out, why doesn't her new lover, Kyle, do it for her? Does my Grandma Amanda know that the dogs pooped all over the house? It was hard for me to sleep that night. I could hear the dog paws clicking all over the house, sounds coming from my mother's room, and the smell was giving me a headache. I shifted my feet from underneath the blanket and crept off the cot to go to the bathroom. After I was done peeing, I reached over to grab some toilet paper, and the cardboard roll stared back at me. I scooted off the seat and waddled over to the cupboard. There was no toilet paper under the sink. It must be somewhere else. I ended up just pulling my underwear up, letting the drops of urine seep into my underwear. It was too dark to look for toilet paper tonight, so I just crept back over to the cot and counted slowly in my head, waiting for morning.

I woke up from the light shining through the crooked curtain. Mom was still asleep and probably would be until lunchtime like usual. The house didn't smell so bad this morning. My nose must have gotten used to the smell. I saw Trudy sleeping on the couch; her arm was dangling off. I let her sleep. I tiptoed my way back down the hall. I was too curious not to investigate the forbidden room. There was a cloud of stench as soon as I pulled the door open. I thought I was going to throw up right there on the floor. Even through my now watery eyes, I could see piles of clothes stacked up. There were avalanches of sludge cascading and crusted over the clothes. There were coiled-up turds smeared onto the carpet and squished into the bedsheets. There were Barbie arms reaching out from mounds of poop, like a zombie arm coming back out of the grave. There must have been at least 50 piles of poop in here. I sealed the room back up. I wouldn't be going back in there again.

I still hadn't let out my morning pee. I wanted to go real quick, but I remembered last minute, there wasn't any toilet paper. I hurried over to the hallway closet, but none in there. I scurried to the kitchen and looked under the sink. None in there. Not only that but by seeing all of those turds in my room, I was working one up myself. I wouldn't be able to clench much longer, and there was sweat gathering in my butt crack from doing so. I was going to have to just go and hope I overlooked it last night. One plop later, the deed was done, but to no surprise, there wasn't even a scrap of toilet paper. I reached into a box of menstrual pads, unwrapped the thin plastic, and wiped my backside off. The pad stuck to my fingertips, and I got poop on my hand trying to get it off. I flicked it in the trash and felt lucky there was soap by the faucet.

Wandering back into the kitchen, I thought about making breakfast for me and Trudy. Dishes lined the counters; gnats swarmed the plates and old yogurt cups. I lost my appetite. I would just wait until she woke up. By the time she did, we decided to just eat peanut butter crackers and fruit snacks. I turned the TV on low volume, and we watched cartoons until my mom woke up around 1 pm. Each day that week felt like an eternity. I didn't have any new clothes to change into, my hair didn't get brushed, and I was growing fur on my teeth because she didn't even have a toothbrush for me. Even though I felt absolutely dirty, I didn't want to shower here. What would be the point? I would just have to put back on my piss-scented underwear.

I was never brave enough to ask her why she slept all day. Why wouldn't she clean up after the dogs? Why she wouldn't clean the house? Why she wouldn't buy the things we needed? Why she wouldn't just take care of me for once in her fucking life?! I just stared at my legs the whole car ride back to meet my dad. Even though we weren't quite ready to move into our new house, it would be better than this.

As soon as my seatbelt was buckled, I told my dad I never wanted to go back there again. There was no bedroom, no toilet paper, barely any food, and she just slept most of the time. I told him about Kyle. I told him my mother said they were going to get married. He just shook his head. We locked eyes in that rear-view mirror, and I could see the pity smeared across his eyebrows.

By next weekend we are going to be completely moved into our new house. Cara and dad have been moving boxes and furniture room by room this week. Grandma Judith and Grandpa John are helping. My new room is the best. Cara and dad surprised us with new beds, bigger beds. They picked out paintings to hang in each of our rooms. Ella has horses; Zack has a gorilla with headphones on, and I…I got a sweet dolphin leaping gracefully out of the water. This is just the best surprise. It goes perfectly with the pink walls and the white sheets and blanket.

This house is so much better than our last house. Not only do we all get our own rooms, but there are 3 bathrooms (all stocked with toilet paper), not just one that we all have to share. You can be in the kitchen and look right into the living room. All of the new furniture leans back, and it's made out of leather, so when you sit down, you don't get Chief's hair all over your butt anymore. There is a little room next to the kitchen. Dad says he's not sure what we will put in there yet. It has the biggest basement I have ever seen. It has a little hiding place underneath the stairs. The backyard doesn't have a fence like our old house. It has so many trees, like our own enchanted forest.

Just when I think things couldn't get any better than this new house, dad says they have another surprise for us. Ella thinks it is a horse. She wants a real live horse so badly. A black one with long hair she can braid. She wants to name it Majesty. It's not a horse, and thank goodness, it's not a new boyfriend. We are going to go to Florida. We are going to drive down, and we will get to drive through the mountains. Zack has been to Florida before, but Ella and I haven't. Cara says we will stay in a house with its own pool for us to swim in. We are going to go to the ocean. I secretly wish I could see a dolphin, but I definitely don't want to see a shark. They say they will have another surprise for us while we are down there, but we have to wait. I don't think I can wait!

Chapter Six: Sugar and Spice and Everything Nice

The L's

There are a few other kids in our Cul-de-sac. There is a brother and sister that live right next door. The brother is in my grade; we will both be going to middle school in the fall. The sister is in Ella's grade. They already know each other from school and soccer. Ella feels relieved that she already knows someone in the neighborhood. It makes me feel excluded and alone. It's not like Ella wouldn't invite me to play with them. It's that she already knows Ella and likes Ella. I will be the third wheel, and she might not even like me. She might just let me hang out with them out of pity.

Poor Ava doesn't have any friends. She has to hang out with her sister because no one even likes her. Ava isn't good enough to have friends. There is something weird about her. There is something off. Ella is better than Ava. Trudy is better than Ava.

There are a few other kids in the cul-de-sac. Some older, some younger, some I have seen in the halls, but have never had the guts to talk to. The best kids in the neighborhood by far are the ones just furthest down the road. The triple threat, if you will. The L's. They live down the other end of the cul-de-sac in a house that is just slightly better than ours. We call them the L's because they all have names that start with the letter L. Laura, Lillian, and Layla. They have a brother, Lucas, but he's not important in my story.

The first time we met them, it was like an interrogation. They wanted to know everything about us. Where did we come from? What school do we go to? How old are we? Do we like peanuts in our M&Ms or not? They have been home-schooled this whole time. They don't have any friends that aren't related to them. Their mom doesn't work and gets to stay home every day to raise them. She's really nice and pretty. Lauren looks a lot like her mom. They are both pretty. Their dad works a lot. They all go to a church that is nearby. It sounds like a lot of fun. They get to play games and listen to music there. There is always a food buffet, and they have a gymnasium where you can play on mats or shoot basketballs. We found out that they were at the Yogi Bear camp at the same time we were last year. I think I remember playing with them on the playground. Layla was kind of bossy.

Lauren: She's the oldest. A whopping 12 years old. Petite and sweet. She's just about 5 foot tall and everyone is sure that she isn't going to get any bigger than that. For as short as she is, her legs look long. Her hair falls, light brown to blond, just below her shoulders. She's thin and wears shirts that show just the bottom of her stomach. She likes fashion, nails, and softball. She has been playing for a softball team for a while. She also learned to ride horses through her online schooling. The school pairs with another program for elective or extracurricular activities. She wants to be a vet when she gets older or maybe a nurse. She's smart and barely even tries at school. She is active with the youth group at her church and helps to watch the children in the daycare section. She's good with kids. I can tell she is shy and has a gentle nature.

Lillian: She's my age, 10. She isn't shy like Lauren but tends to keep to herself. She doesn't wear makeup yet. She has brown hair that goes to her shoulder blades. She wears tie-dye t-shirts and supportive sandals, not flip-flops like the rest of us. She also plays softball, but you can tell sports aren't as important to her as they are to her sisters. She likes to do activities that most people would do alone, like reading. She says she's not quite sure what she wants to be when she gets older, but I feel like she will be a loner, not in a bad way. She's brilliant enough to be a groundbreaking scientist but also a little morbid, just enough that she could be a Mortician. She's definitely the more cautious sister, and she's like the "mom" sister of the group. She's not too serious, though, and she makes everyone laugh. She has an infectious smile. I like that about her. It makes me want to smile. It makes me want to be happy inside, too.

Layla: She's the youngest, sitting at just 9 years old. She is bold and outgoing. A right in your face whether you want her to be or not, girl. She has short blond hair, parted in the middle and slicked to the sides of her face. She is wearing just a plain red crew cut t-shirt with a lifeguard symbol on it with jean shorts. She is thin and awkward, standing there like she just got legs for the first time, fidgeting her feet around. She has scabbed-up legs, and you can tell she plays outside all the time. She's not scared to get her hands dirty. She is a wild child. She's loud and funny. She's an in-your-face kind of person; type A, you might say. I imagine her being a big-time event planner for celebrities or a high-end realtor. She may be the youngest, but she is in charge of the pack. I can feel the energy around her. She likes sports, makeovers, and movies. I can tell that she really likes mischief just by the way that she smiles. I fell in love with her immediately.

They invited us to their house. They invited themselves into our house. They told us they knew the kids that lived here before us, and they were bad kids. They told us that they had a dog, too, but it was a special dog. The little girl that lived here before, who stayed in Ella's room, was diabetic, and the dog could wake her up in the night if her sugars were too low. There were two brothers, but they were always doing weird stuff. Sometimes, they would just go back and start hitting the trees and brush with axes and things, not really cutting anything down. They just liked hitting things, I guess. They wanted to see what the house looked like inside. They weren't allowed in it before we moved here. They wanted to see if the rumors were true. If there was a grandma ghost that haunted the halls. It freaked me out, and I wondered if the grandma really died in our house. Which room was her room? Hopefully not mine.

They were quite the little detectives and pointed out a bunch of remnants of the previous owners than we had even noticed. In Ella's closest, the little girl had drawn a smiling face on the wall. Cara says she tried to paint it over several times, but it just kept smiling through. On the basement doors were ruler marks, measuring each kid as they grew taller. We didn't find any evidence of a ghost, and that was what I was worried the most about. I didn't need anything else haunting me.

They know all of the gossip about the neighborhood. They go down the line of houses and tell us something weird or off about each house. The couple directly next to us is not really married; they just live together, and the mom goes by a different name. Apparently, her name is Sherry, but it's an old person's name, so she goes by an alias. The guy across from them has his own lawn care business, but the girls are positive they hear scratching and whispers from the back of his trailer. Probably have kids locked in there. The old couple on the corner is super nice to your face but gives off creepy vibes, too eager to invite you into their house. Kiddie corner to that house, a now single mom and her two kids live there. Apparently, the dad was a teacher at a different school district and got caught being intimate with a student. Went to prison. The lady two houses down from that has agoraphobia.

I loved the L's right away. Since they lived so close, we could walk back and forth to each other's houses all day long to hang out. Cara and dad said they could trust their parents, so we were allowed to have sleepovers. Their mom was sweet. She didn't work so she could take care of the house and the kids. Their dad had like three jobs and worked as a nurse practitioner. You could never be too sure, though, and after hearing about the other dad down the road, the one in prison, Cara said if something seemed off, let her know right away.

I was over the moon about moving into this house. Dakota used to live close, but we were never allowed to stay over at her house. Cara knew her dad went to school with him. She said he was okay but felt leery about her other siblings and didn't know his live-in girlfriend very well. Dakota could sometimes stay at our house, but it wasn't the same.

We wanted to impress the L's so badly. We told them that we were going to go to Florida in a few weeks. Apparently, they had just gotten back from Florida. Layla took a lot of pictures while they were in Florida. She has pictures of the ocean, sunset, and palm trees. There were so many palm trees. She tried to climb one, got abrasions on her thighs, and scratched her toe. She was only 9, but she already had her very own phone. I never wanted a phone until I met Layla.

I felt like I could tell them anything. But I didn't. I didn't tell them anything about my life before living with Liam. I didn't even tell them that Cara wasn't my mom for a long time because I didn't want them to ask about my real one. I didn't want them to know that she left me. I really didn't want to give them a reason to feel like there was something wrong with me. So, I kept all those secrets and memories buried deep in the back of my mind, and Pinkie promised myself that I would never bring that up in front of them. Of course, that didn't last too long. It was hard to explain that I had to go somewhere else every other weekend without explaining that it was to visit with my mom. Luckily, most of the time, if I just asked, she would let me stay at Liam's. She had a lot going on anyway.

They were getting ready to go to church camp for a few weeks. I didn't want them to go. I wished I had a phone even more now so I could talk to Layla while she was at camp. What if they made friends while they were there and didn't want to be friends with us when they got back? Would they miss me like I was going to miss them?

Right before they left for camp, they broke the more exciting news to us. They were going to go to school this fall. They were going to go to our school. That meant we could ride the bus together every morning. I felt less worried about losing them now. It would have been miserable to be without them and have to go back to my mom's trailer, too.

My dad spoke to my mom after I begged him not to make me go. Cara said we could just pack my backpack with things I would need, like a toothbrush, or she could just give my mom money to buy one. I told her no. This would just make things worse for me there. My mom did NOT like it when I told my dad "bad" things about her. I was glad to hear that she said I could stay here, but at the same time, I felt disappointed that she didn't even put up a little fight. She was perfectly happy without me there. She has Kyle and Trudy, after all. I bet she even gave my cot to Trudy.

Chapter Seven: Sunshine and Alligators

The drive to Florida was a long one. I mostly slept on the way down. We were kind of cramped in the back seat. Ella is the smallest, so she sat in the middle. Cara let us all pick out ten of our favorite songs, and she put them all together on a drive that we could listen to in the Jeep for the trip. Dad is so funny when he starts singing to girl music. He acts like he is singing into a microphone, and then he sings the words wrong. He's so silly, and we all laugh. He says he thought the words were actually "bacon and eggs" instead of "thank you, next". Speaking of food, we stopped off and tried new restaurants. Cara says she doesn't want to eat anywhere on this trip that she could have eaten back home. They let us get snacks and slushies from the gas station. We drove through the mountains in Kentucky and Tennessee. They were amazing. I was a little scared that the rocks would fall and hit us, crushing the car. Small pieces and larger chunks of the mountain scattered the edges of the highway that we drove down. Some areas even had nets in place to catch the falling rocks.

It was also scary driving through Georgia. The highway was about 8 lanes across, and everyone was driving so fast. There were literally large signs that stretched out above the highway telling you how many people had already died on it that year. I think it was supposed to make people feel more cautious, but no one speeding passed us seemed to care. I'm glad that I am not grown up yet and I don't have to drive. I didn't want to get into a car accident before we even got to see the palm trees.

When we finally made it to Florida, we stopped at the Welcome Center. Even the air down here smells so much sweeter than the air back in Indiana. Cara let us have cups of orange juice at the Welcome Center. We took a picture under the sign that says, "Welcome to the Sunshine State" and sent it to Grandma Judith and Grandpa John to let them know that we had made it down. Even though we made it to Florida, we still had a few hours to drive. Dad says we are going to a town called Kissimmee. It looks like someone is asking for a kiss, like please kiss-uh-me, but Cara says it's pronounced a little different. It is close to Orlando. Dad says it is too busy in Orlando. The highway is backed up, and cars are bumper to bumper in the lane that says Disney World above it.

When we got to the neighborhood, the houses were painted beautiful colors. They were not the old greys, tans, and blues like the houses back in Indiana. There were even some houses that were bubble gum pink. When we got to the house, it had so many bedrooms. Even here on vacation, we would all get our own rooms. The pool was so big. It was enclosed in a sunroom. My dad says that all the pools in Florida have to have a fence or something around them because nobody wants to wake up to a gator in their pool.

Even though we had just got there, dad let us change into our bathing suits right away. We didn't even have to unpack yet. We were all too excited to go swimming. We were running and jumping in. Cara made up a game where someone would make a special move and then leap into the pool, and we would all have to copy them and jump in, too. Dad floated around on a unicorn floaty, and we tried swimming underneath him. We snuck up on the side of the floaty and squirted him with squirt guns and water from the pool noodles. We swam until we were soggy.

We got up early and drove down to a secluded dock. We were going on an airboat. I have never seen a boat like this before. It had a giant fan on the back of it, and it went really fast. Dad's hat blew off his head from how fast we were going. He couldn't jump into the water to get it because we were in a marsh. The alligators lived in the marsh. The tour guide circled back and used a long pole to grab it for him. He said he knew where we could see baby alligators. We went really slow and came across the nest. There were lots of tiny little alligators swimming around. I wondered where the mother alligator was. I wondered if she was getting them something to eat or if she abandoned them. I wanted to pick up one of the tiny alligators, pet and love him. The tour guide said they have razor-sharp teeth. I decided I didn't want to pet one after all.

It seemed like there were a lot of alligator things to do in Florida. The next day, we went to a place called Gator Land. It was kind of like a Zoo for alligators. There were a few big cats there and small, funny-looking animals called Capybaras. Of course, there were lots of alligators. They had baby alligators all the way up to old men alligators. They even had an all-white alligator. We bought food that looked like freeze-dried turds and threw them off a boardwalk into the water and watched the alligators all snap their jaws to get them. We saw two big male alligators fighting each other and biting each other's faces. I'm glad Ella and I don't fight like that. Ella would probably try to eat one of my eyeballs.

I felt like an alligator. When we weren't hanging out around them, we were home swimming in the pool and bathing in the sun. What a life. After seeing the alligators, Ella and I pretended we were alligators and were practicing our death rolls in the pool. It was tiring. We got to hunt prey, too. Well, sort of. There were a bunch of little lizards that ran around the grass and up the sides of the house. They were fast, but we caught a bunch of them.

Dad took us to go see dinner shows. We went to the Arcade, played glow-in-the-dark mini golf, and drove around in Go Karts. Ella and I got to drive our own Go Karts and acted like we were racing in Mario Kart. Zack and dad got to drive in fast Go Karts on an indoor track where they had to wear helmets. Dad said I could try driving on the indoor track, too, but I didn't like the way the cars went that fast. I was scared someone would scrape my car and send me flying across the track. It seemed much more extreme than the bumper cars at the fair, where you just get jostled a little. We all got to buy a souvenir and a T-shirt. Cara let us take all kinds of photos on her phone. I wanted to show Layla all the fun things that we got to do.

The surprise we had all been waiting for was that they were taking us to Universal Studios. Zack didn't like Disney princesses, so Cara thought this would be better. We watched movies and rode on roller coasters and in things called simulators. They had all kinds of cool rides: Minions, Jurassic Park, Harry Potter, Simpsons, Incredible Hulk, Transformers, and someone named the Terminator. Cara couldn't believe Ella, and I didn't know who the Terminator was: Arnold Schwarzenegger, the legend himself. We were there so long that my feet hurt, and my belly was full of all the treats they bought for us. Before it could even get dark out, Ella and I were complaining about having to walk any further. Taking turns to have dad put us on his back for a little while. Zack was starting to get tall. I would have laughed to see him on dad's back. I wonder if his shoes would have dragged across the ground.

We only stayed one more day in Florida after that. Then, it was back home to Indiana. Cara bought us puzzle books for the way home so we wouldn't get so bored. I napped for most of the way home. We went through all the pictures we had taken, and I mentally categorized the best ones to show Layla as soon as we got back.

Once we got home, summer was coming to an end. I wasn't sad about having to go back to school. Not this year. I had many new friends to go back to school with and hang out with once it was over. Lillian was in my grade and could help me study for homework and tests.

Dad bought us an electric golf cart that summer. He let us drive it all over the cul-de-sac. He made us take turns driving because he didn't want anyone hogging it the whole time. Layla was wild. She would turn the wheel so sharply, the pedal pushed completely to the floor, that I thought we would definitely flip the golf cart. On the first day, Ella ran it straight into a tree. It didn't do any damage to the cart; it just gave everyone a little bit of whiplash. Well, I actually flew off the back into a pile of rocks, but no broken bones, just a spilled Mountain Dew.

I have one more week that I will have to go to my mom's house. Dad says my Grandma Amanda told him that my mom moved out of her trailer. The one with the dog poop everywhere. My mom didn't have a phone anymore, so Amanda had to tell my dad. When I was eavesdropping upstairs, I heard him tell Cara that my mother had been evicted from the trailer. It sounded like she was going to have to move back in with my Grandma Amanda until she could find another trailer to live in. I could tell by the strain in his voice that he was getting fed up with my mother. He was fed up with her constant moving and choosing not to settle down and get a job.

He was fed up with her not being able to take care of me. He didn't like sending me to dirty houses without "real food".

I later found out she left that dump of a trailer alright. She never cleaned it up; she literally just walked away. Left all the shit-covered clothes and clutter for someone else to deal with. If you haven't already read enough to feel infuriated by her, I want you to know that she left the dogs. She left them in the deserted trailer without food or water. Left them to wander around in their own feces. Someone tipped off animal control. I have a suspicion it was my Grandma Amanda, and they were able to rescue them. If only saving a child was as simple. She lucked out and wasn't charged with animal cruelty, neglect, or abandonment. She was getting really lucky about getting away with those types of offenses.

Chapter Eight: Camp Highland

11 Years Old

Sixth grade blew right by. It was such a great year. The L's were phenomenal friends. Each girl was a little bit different but completely spectacular in their own way. I thought about Layla all the time. We even talked Cara into letting us ride with them to school every day instead of riding on the bus. We could head over early in the morning and get ready together. We could do each other's hair and makeup while we gossiped about other kids at school before the day had even begun. That school year, I could even mend my friendship with Dakota.

Sixth grade, riding on the confidence I mirrored from Layla, I had tried out for sideline cheerleading. Of course, Ella also did cheer. *Copycat.* The L's weren't doing cheer, so it was nice to have someone to go to cheer camp with. Someone to complain about how hot it was and, of course, someone to make fun of the other girls with. Cara spent the weekends driving us around to various schools, watching us cheer on the crowd. Ella and I would practice those cheers over and over in the car. I'm pretty sure Cara knew all the chants before the first week of the season.

It was fun getting "all dolled up", Cara doing our hair and

painting our nails blue and white for the games. Placing the bow delicately into our hair. It was fun shaking the pom poms around and practicing high kicks and cartwheels. I would always get so nervous at the games, though. I didn't want the people in the crowds to stare at me.

What if I messed up? What if I stomped when I was supposed to clap? What if I forgot the words to cheer? What if I wasn't good enough to be on the team? What if I embarrassed myself? Would Cara be disappointed in me? Would she be mad that she drove all this way just for me to mess up? Sometimes, I would just do the movements and lip sync to the cheers. Sometimes, I would just whisper the words so if I messed up, no one would know. I decided that after this season, I wouldn't take the risk of embarrassing myself with cheerleading anymore.

I left those cheer worries back in the sixth grade. It was summer again. The best thing about summer was that my Grandma Amanda bought me a phone. My dad said that I was too young to have one, but I begged my Grandma Amanda to get me one, and she did. Now I could text Layla all the time. It turns out that was hardly needed, considering we were always with each other. She was just so much fun, and I wanted to be just like her. I started dressing and acting like her, even talking like her.

Since spring, her dad had a pool installed in their backyard.

It was finally done, and he put a fence up around it, even though there weren't any gators in Indiana. It had a diving board and a slide. We wouldn't even have to go to Florida to swim. The best part was because we were all best friends now, we would get to swim all summer long. Ella and I basically lived there in the summer. We spent most of the nights sleeping over. We sometimes stayed at our house too, especially when we wanted to watch scary movies and things that they weren't allowed to do at their house. We would just come to our house and sneakily do it anyway.

Because I had my own phone now, I was able to start calling and texting my mom that I didn't want to come for my weekend visits and especially didn't want to go to my weeklong visits. She just let me stay here. I dreaded when my dad would make us stay home from the girl's house. He said we didn't need to stay there every night and that sometimes he wanted to see us, too. Cara joked that if we stayed there that much, they would have to add us to their family portrait that hung in their living room. I wouldn't have minded that at all. I felt like we were way more than friends. I felt like we were all sisters. I could change my name from Ava to something else, something like Lacey, you know, something with an L.

Dad was working a lot and getting forced to stay over at work. Cara was working at the hospital in the ER, so she was home more often than he was. She only had to work 3 days per week. On her days off, she would take us all to the zoo and the movies. She would buy us lunch from restaurants and bake fresh cookies for us to eat. She stocked up on water and Caprisuns for us to grab to and from each other's houses. She didn't really fuss about us being gone all the time. She said we were kids and deserved to have a good time in the summer. She said the girl's house was like a camp. Camp Highland, she called it (Highland was their last name).

It basically was a summer camp. We did a lot of swimming, bonding, crafts, picture taking, and games. We did a lot of sun tanning. We rode around on the golf cart and took turns riding the hoverboards and penny boards down the street. Dad and Cara bought us a new trampoline for this backyard and a basketball hoop for the front. The girls also had a trampoline. Somehow, their trampoline just seemed better than ours. We would bounce each other around and try not to jump on each other's faces. Ella and I even started going to church with the girls some of the evenings. We talked Layla's mom into driving us all around as well. She would take us ice skating, bowling, and to the movies, too.

It was crazy how our parents would think so much alike. The girl's parents were planning to take them to Tennessee this year for vacation. That was exactly where we were going this year, too. I wished we were going at the same time so we could convince them to get one house for all of us. It would be so boring without Layla here. Ella was fine and all, but Layla was exciting.

While they were gone on vacation, my Grandma Amanda was making me feel guilty for not coming to see her. She said that she wouldn't pay for my phone anymore if I didn't visit her. I took advantage of Layla being gone to go ahead and visit my grandma. My little sister Trudy was living there now. She was so annoying. She wasn't anything like Ella. She didn't let me be the boss of her. We had to share a room at my grandma's house because my uncle had to move back in with his girlfriend and kid, too. Trudy was always taking my things and ruining my makeup. I couldn't talk on the phone without her eavesdropping on me and trying to overhear my secrets. I could feel that I wasn't my Grandma Amanda's favorite anymore. She used to fawn over me. I used to get whatever I wanted at her house and get ALL the attention. Now, my grandma was stretched thin. There were so many cousins running around. She had to take care of everyone's kids and couldn't pay attention to just me anymore.

On the last night of the week that I would be there, they invited over lots of family members, and we were going to have a bonfire. All the adults were drinking. I ended up having to help watch all the kids and tried to entertain them. I heard all kinds of stories as the night went on. My grandma's brother was going to be getting out of prison soon. I heard the adults fussing over him. Saying he was a pedophile. Saying that he wasn't supposed to be around the children, so he probably wouldn't be able to come visit her when he got out of prison because so many kids lived at her house now. I heard my grandpa hassling my mom, asking her when she was going to get her shit together. He said she needed to get a job and needed to quit mooching off them. He was tired of having to raise her kids. I heard my uncle say that he was going to try to get custody of his kids, but it would be hard because he didn't have a job either and was living with his mom.

While eavesdropping was fun because you could learn a lot of secrets, it made me glad I didn't live here anymore. There was always something wrong and someone complaining about something. About that time, one of my mom's cousins had completely lost it. Next thing we know, she is hysterical and crying. She is screaming that she hates herself and she is such a burden to everybody. She might as well be dead. She started screaming that she was going to kill herself. She was trying to run away down the driveway, and everyone was trying to catch her and calm her down. It made me feel scared. I didn't want to see her kill herself. I had to act like an adult now, even though these ones didn't know how to act themselves. I just ushered my little sister and cousins closer to the house to look for fireflies. I didn't want them to have to witness something like this. I didn't want them to start having nightmares like I do.

My mom told me not to tell my dad. She said he wouldn't understand, and he would try to make a big deal out of it. I kind of felt like someone screaming they wanted to kill themselves was serious, but my mom assured me that she wouldn't do it. She just says it for attention. She says some people just need attention, so they do crazy things to get it. I told her I wouldn't tell my dad. That was a lie, though. I was most definitely going to tell my dad because I learned a long time ago that when you had stories like this, stories about terrible things that happened, you got people's attention. When I told my dad things like this, he would get upset. Cara didn't understand why he had to keep sending me to see my mom because "something crazy" always happened. She felt like it wasn't safe for me to keep going there.

Poor Ava. Everyone always feels bad for Ava. Such a pity.

It felt like there was no time at all between the girls coming back from Tennessee and us leaving to go. The time we spent in Tennessee was nothing short of amazing. We stayed in a cabin that was high up in the mountains and had an amazing view. In the mornings, you could watch the mountains smoke. We got to do so many activities there. We went to dinner shows in Tennessee just like we did in Florida. We got to walk around the town. We got to ride a roller coaster in the mountains.

I think my favorite thing that we did was go horseback riding. I was scared to get on an adult horse. I had only been on ponies at the fair. I was even scared of that. The horse was so good, though. My dad's horse was a little crazier. I think it must have eaten something that made its tummy feel sick because it kept farting in front of the rest of us. My dad even tried farting and blaming it on the horse. Even though my dad was making us laugh on his horse, I also felt calm. Once I overcame my initial fear, I felt lucky to trot along with such an amazing animal. I liked stroking his head as he carried me up the mountain to thank him for not throwing me off into the mud. Now I know why Ella liked horses so much.

When we got back from Tennessee, the girls were already off to church camp. I tried to convince dad to let me go with them to the camp this summer. He wouldn't let me go because we were going to be in Tennessee. Luckily, I got invited to a sleepover birthday party with some of my other friends from school. Dakota was going to be there, so I decided to go too. This friend did not live in a nice house like ours. When my dad dropped me off, her dad answered the door without a shirt on with this pot belly sticking out and covered with a trail of hair. I didn't bother telling my dad that her mom didn't live here. I should have known then that this was going to be quite the sleepover, not like sleeping over at Layla's house.

When I got home the next day, I couldn't wait to tell Ella and Cara about what happened at the birthday party. The birthday girl was more like a birthday cat. When we all filed upstairs into her bedroom, her room was kind of dirty like the rest of her house. We were dancing and singing along to music when out of nowhere, she walked over to the corner of the room and dropped both her shorts and underwear, squatted down, and pissed right there on the carpet, right in front of everyone. Dakota and I locked eyes immediately. Why didn't she cover up her vagina while hot urine squirted into the beige fibers? Who does something like that? She didn't even seem bothered by it. In fact, looking around at her carpet, it looked like she did it all the time. She didn't even wipe; she just slid her bottoms back up. I was hoping that she wasn't going to have to poop that night.

Later, we were all kind of getting thirsty, but she didn't have anything to drink other than tap water at her house. Her dad was snoring in the chair in the living room. She woke him up and asked him if he would take us down to the gas station to get something to drink. Not only would he not take us, but he told her that she would have to spend her birthday money to get it and that she would have to walk down there. My dad would never let us walk to a gas station at night. Dakota and I decided that we would stay back at her house while they went. The upstairs bathroom was bare and disgusting. Apparently, she did sometimes use the toilet because there was urine marinating in the water. The bathtub curtain was pulled back, and black grime was caked onto the sides of the tub. There were sprinkles of toothpaste bedazzling the mirror. Her dad's room was just down the hall. Even though he wasn't in it, I got an eerie feeling about even getting close to the door. The inside of her house was starting to freak us out. We imagined the shapes and shadows on the walls as something more sinister. We opted to stay outside. We were going to lie on the trampoline, but this was not like Layla's house. There was a huge hole ripping through it. We just sat anxiously on the back steps until they came back.

It was hard to sleep that night. Some of the lucky kids got to sleep on the mattress with Mindy. The unlucky few of us had to sleep on the pee-stained floor. There weren't any spare blankets, but there were some sheets. It was fridged lying on the floor. Dakota and I laid back-to-back, sharing the thin twin-sized sheet. It wasn't like I imagined that if your body got cold enough, you would slowly drift off into hibernation. My muscles ached, and my body attempted to shiver to create heat. This was not like Layla's house at all.

I told Ella and Cara the story. I embellished it just a little. They laughed at the funny parts I added, like they were going to pee themselves. They were shocked and in disbelief when I told them the other parts. Cara said I could not stay the night there ever again. She mulled over the idea of calling CPS just to check things out. She says sometimes kids just need someone to advocate for them. I told her after that night, I was not sure if I wanted to be friends with Mindy anymore. I didn't know she was such a weirdo. She acts normal at school, and she definitely does not pee in the hallways. Cara said it was fine if I didn't want to hang out with her, but she advised me not to go around telling other kids or making fun of her. She said she obviously had some psychological problems and I shouldn't make things worse for her.

Once Ella went upstairs, I told Cara that it reminded me of my mom's trailer. The one with the dog poop everywhere. It made me sad for her. Mindy's home life reminded me of what mine would have been like if I had had to stay with my mother. At least I only had to endure short periods in those conditions. She had to live like that all the time. Her mother left them when she was very young. She had an older sister, but she left that house as soon as she was able. I don't blame her. But I pity Mindy for having to live like that. I didn't realize it was so common for a mother to just leave her children. This is what it must feel like for Liam and Cara when they send me to my mother's house: feeling helpless because there isn't much you can do, feeling pity for the child. At that moment, we shared a brief instance of silence, a minute dedicated to pity, mine for Mindy and Cara's for me.

Chapter Nine: Best Friends, Basketball, and Betrayal

7ᵗʰ Grade

Ella made the three of us, her, Layla, and me, BFF bracelets out of a little bracelet-making kit she got for Christmas. This made it official. Layla was my best friend. Even though we had no classes or lunch together, she was the best part about the school. Sometimes, people waved or talked to me because I knew Layla. She was popular, so I was gaining popularity myself just by being seen with her. Lillian was in my grade, but we had no classes together. She was scheduled for lunch at the same time I was, but we sat at different tables. It would have been easy to be best friends with Lillian, but I really just wanted to be friends with Layla.

I don't really like that Layla wants to be best friends with both me and Ella. It makes me feel jealous to have to share Layla with anyone else. But I pretend it doesn't bother me because I would rather share Layla than worry about if she would choose me. I don't want to be alone. I don't want her to leave me.

Sometimes, Layla wants to do things that I don't want to do, but I do them anyway. Like sometimes, after we get out of the pool and I have already showered and redressed, Layla decides she wants to get back in, so we do. Sometimes, even when I am wearing real clothes and not my bathing suit, she will just push me into the pool, clothes and all, and I just pretend that I am not mad. Sometimes, Layla wants to play fight, but she takes it too far. She pushes me down and slaps me on the head and face. It makes me feel weak and embarrassed. Instead of telling her this, I just laugh it off. That is just how Layla is, right? She tells me that we don't eat fries warm. We don't dip our fries in ketchup because that is gross, so we eat them plain. We also don't show our toes anymore. We only wear tall black Nike socks (not Under Armor or Adidas) and slides now. We also have an obsession with hoodies.

As I've said, Layla is popular. She has lots of friends. When she is hanging out with her softball friends or even just having another girl from school over, I secretively hope she invites me over anyway because we are best friends. If I can't coax her into inviting me, I pretend to want to hang out with Lillian so that I can go down to their house. Once I'm there, I make up excuses to try to spy on Layla anyway. I tell Lillian I am going to use the bathroom and really just wander down the hall with my ear pressed against the wood of Layla's door, listening to her laughter. If she's not in her room, I will go downstairs "to get a drink or a snack." I try to act surprised when I see Layla and another friend. I want to make her jealous as she makes me. I told her I didn't know she was home and I was just hanging out with Lillian. It burns me when she says things like, "ok, have fun." I try to contain my excitement when Lillian suggests that we "crash" their party and go hang out with Layla and her friends.

I decided that I must not be sporty enough for Layla. Lillian is going to try out for the basketball. She asked me to try out for the team with her. I have dribbled a ball before. It can't be that hard, right? Just try to get the ball inside the hoop. I was wrong. I didn't even know what a layup was before today, and I was supposed to do one for the coach in front of everyone else. I could have died right there on the spot. My heart was thudding out of my chest, and it wasn't just from the laps that we did to warm up. The sweat on my brow was solely from my anxiety. I also realized that shooting a three-pointer was harder than it looked. The line is much further away than it looks on TV. I am good at blocking. I'm not bad at free throws. So, at least, I have that going for me.

If Layla wouldn't have told me how cool it was to be trying out for the basketball team, I wouldn't have even gone to the second day of tryouts. I would have pretended to be sick and just let Lillian down. After tryouts, the coach would post a list the next day telling us which team we were on. The A team or the B team. Apparently, there were not enough girls that tried out to have to make cuts. I was thankful for that. I didn't need to even look at the list to know that I was going to be on the B team. I just wanted to see what team Lillian was going to be on. Whether or not Layla complimented me for being on the basketball team, I would not participate if Lillian ended up on the A team. I didn't know any of the other girls on the team, and I didn't want to. For now, Layla was enough for me.

The next day, Lillian and I stayed after school and met in the gymnasium. Lillian was also in the B Team. Relief. The coach met everyone in the locker room, passing out the jerseys and shorts. They were all baggy. I looked ridiculous. But if this would make Layla like me more, I was going to do it. I would play my hardest if Layla would just come to watch me play, which was very likely considering her sister was on the team. We practiced three nights a week after school, which meant I could ride home with her at least 3 days a week if she came with her mom to pick up her sister.

Back at home, dad was getting mandated less. Cara was still working at the hospital, but since school started this fall, she also re-enrolled in school, graduate school. She was working on getting her master's degree. She was going to take all her didactic classes online and then, over the next year, start finding local clinicals to finish. Zack was in his junior year now and was taking Criminal Justice courses through the Career Center on top of the normal high school curriculum. Ella didn't have anything specific going on that year. She still played fall and spring soccer but didn't do any other after-school activities. Dad was still able to make it to my games. Cara came to just a few, but she was able to make the home ones usually. With Zack and Ella not being in any sports right now, it was kind of nice being the center of attention for our household. Dad offered to practice out front with me, but I didn't want Ryan from across the street to see me playing with my dad; hanging out with parents was for losers. Rumor had it that he liked one of us, either me or Layla. I didn't like Ryan, really. He was short and rude. That's not a good combination. The idea of someone liking me more than Layla made me like him. I wanted it to be me.

If I was going to be the center of attention now, with boys possibly liking me, I was going to have to start working harder on my appearance. I started wearing my hair parted in the middle, slicked down to the sides like Layla. I let her show me how to shave my legs. I was almost 12 years old. I'm not sure what age you can start shaving your legs, but I didn't want to ask Cara. What if she said I was too young? No, I would shave my legs secretly at Layla's house under her guidance. She also told me that we were supposed to shave our arms, so I let her shave my forearms. During one sleepover, everyone watched as Layla suggested that I have a hairy back and I should let her shave that, too.

Later, Dakota said she heard that if you shave hair, it grows back thicker and darker. I feel that Layla was trying to sabotage me. She must have heard that Ryan might like me and wanted to turn me into a gorilla. For the first time, I feel angry with Layla, and not secretly, out loud angry with her. I texted her and accused her of trying to sabotage me. She tells me I am crazy and that shaving my hair won't make it come back thicker. She says I am being crazy. *I am not crazy.* And after that, she didn't respond to me for 3 days. The worst part, at school, Ryan says he doesn't like either one of us. He says we are childish and "not his type." I don't know why I felt like getting attention from a boy was more important than having a friendship with Layla. *It's because your mom does that all the time. She always chooses a man over you.*

An eternity of 72 hours and a hefty apology later, Layla and I agree that we are not going to fight over boys anymore. She still denies that she was trying to sabotage me. She says she was just trying to give me a much-needed makeover.

The following weekend, I was scheduled to go visit my mom. I tried to get out of it, but she told me it was Trudy's birthday, and they were going to have a party. I didn't want to make Trudy feel like I didn't love her, so I decided to go. I told my mom about joining the basketball team. I asked her if she could make a game. They were during the week and not on the weekends. She said she'd think about coming (but she never did). I told her that I had a crush on the boy across the street. She seemed delighted to hear I was interested in boys. She told me that I shouldn't wear hoodies all the time. She said that boys like girls who show little skin. She said I should wear more "form-fitting" clothes, and boys would really notice me then.

She told me she would get me some new shirts and some makeup, too. She said we had to go to the store to pick up a gift for Trudy anyway. She was already at my Grandma Amanda's house. Grandma decorated the house and bought her a Monster High cake and everything.

We never made it to the store. My mom was busy texting on her phone, and she rolled through a stop sign right in front of a cop! He whipped around and pulled her over. He took her license and insurance and went back to the cruiser. After about 15 minutes, a second cruiser showed up. The officers approached the window and informed my mom that she had a warrant for her arrest, a bench warrant for unpaid child support. She was going to have to go to jail. The officer asked if there was anyone who could come pick me up. She told the officer there must be a mistake. She said that she pays my dad's child support in cash every month. He must not have been reporting it to the Friend of the Court. She never thought she would need to ask him for receipts. She promises that she is going to get this cleared right up on Monday morning when Friend of the Court opens. He wasn't buying her story, so she called my Grandma Amanda to come pick me up.

While I was waiting for grandma to arrive, the cops searched through my mom's pockets—nothing but a Bic lighter and a half pack of Newports. The first officer handcuffed her and sat her in the back of the cruiser. They left the door open so she could get some air while they were waiting. The officers explained the situation when my grandma came peeling up. She gave my mom the stink eye and then took my hand. My mom didn't even bother to say sorry or bye to me as I walked over to my grandma's car. She just asked the officer if she could smoke one last cigarette before they closed the door.

We went ahead and had Trudy's party anyway. She didn't seem to notice or care that our mother wasn't there. She was probably used to it by now. I helped hand Trudy presents to unwrap for the crowd. When it came to singing her happy birthday, though, I didn't sing. Even though I should be happy for her, I couldn't. I didn't like that she was getting everyone's attention, and everyone was there just for her. I didn't like that my grandma held her in her lap like she used to hold me.

After the party, my grandma asked me to help clean up. She told me there was a misunderstanding earlier and that I shouldn't worry about my mom. She would help get her out of jail after the weekend after she talked to my pa. I might as well go ahead and stay the weekend with her. She didn't let me call or text my dad for those two days. She said he didn't need to know right away that my mom had gone to jail. She said it wouldn't change anything, but it might worsen my mom's situation. I agreed just so I could enjoy the rest of our alone time, even if it was just picking up wrapping paper and plastic cups from the yard.

When I got home on Sunday, the first thing I saw was Ella wearing one of Layla's sweaters. I was seething inside. Why was she wearing my best friend's sweater? Ella said she had stayed the night there all weekend (without me), and it was cold in the morning after church, so Layla let her borrow it. At that moment, I got a terrible urge to get revenge on Ella. She was painting a picture of the sunset on a small canvas with her acrylic paints. I told her the least she should do was roll up the sleeves so she didn't ruin Layla's sweater with paint. She had paint on her hands and an "oops" look on her face. I offered to help her roll the sleeves myself. I reached over to her wrist, looped my finger under her best friend's bracelet, and yanked it up fast with the sleeve. We watched the string snap and the beads going flying across the floor. She was not Layla's best friend; I was.

Instantly, I swindled her with an apology. I even helped to pick up the multicolor beads and block letters from the floor for her. I told her I would help her make a new one. I didn't want her to tell dad or Cara that I broke her bracelet. If she did, I wanted to make sure she thought that it was a complete accident. I needed to be more careful in the future.

Breaking the bracelet made me feel good inside like I had accomplished something. It felt like the right first step in breaking up their friendship. If it was going to be anyone's job to break up their friendship, it was mine. Best friends are supposed to look out for each other. I was Layla's best friend, and I knew that being friends with Ella wasn't best for her. She didn't have to entertain her just because she was my sister. The wheels started turning in my head.

Chapter Ten: Intrusive Thoughts

12 Years Old: Monsters are not born; they are made.

I don't know how I got here, but here I am—laying in my bed, twirling the edges of my tapestry on my wall. I'm having those thoughts again. The same kind of thoughts that plagued my mind years ago thinking about Dakota and the way she looked at Ella. Like, somehow, Ella was better than me. More fun than me. My little sister was trying to steal Layla from me. Layla was spending the weekends I was gone with my little sister. She was enjoying it. She was sharing videos and Facetiming Ella on her tablet. Even though Ella was one year younger than her, she didn't find her annoying. She liked hanging out with her. Why? Ella didn't dress like her. Ella didn't like the same type of music. Ella didn't follow her around or pretend to like everything that she liked. I was going to have to figure out a way to make Layla forget about Ella.

For the following months, I tried to make Ella out to be a little troll. I wanted her to be ugly, dumb, and weird. I wanted Layla to see her as a pest, a little child that we were too cool to hang around with.

I started by picking on Ella for her appearance. I made fun of the clothes that she wore. I picked on her about her glasses and made sure to make fun of them in front of the L's. "She looks like a grandma. Why are your frames so big? It looks like you got your glasses passed down to you from a grandparent". Ella felt embarrassed. I overheard her asking Cara to buy her different glasses, clear frame glasses, trendier glasses so she could fit in better.

I pointed out that she was gaining weight. I made fun of how her stomach stuck out over her jeans. Ella started feeling bad about her body. She didn't want to wear jeans anymore, only leggings with oversized t-shirts to cover herself. Every time I saw her eating a snack, I would berate her. The things I said to her, a 10-year-old child, would make you sick. I screamed at the top of my lungs how selfish she was. Accused her of eating all the food in the house because she was SO fat.

No, that's the tame version. Have you ever demanded that a child, a 10-year-old child, commit suicide? I have. I screamed at Ella to slit her wrists! I screamed for her just to go dig a hole and then die in it. She should just kill herself! Strictly because she ate the last bag of snack-sized Doritos before I got the chance to eat them myself. I would repeat these commands over and over each time a snack I wanted was gone. I demanded she kill herself because I thought she was getting too fat.

In front of Layla, I made sure to let her know that she was

weighing more than me now, wearing bigger pants than me. I told Layla she couldn't borrow her clothes anymore because Ella was just simply becoming too fat to wear any of them. Liam was so angry after Ella told my dad I was picking on her weight. He told me if he ever heard of me shaming my sister again, he would ground me and take away my "precious" phone. I didn't stop. I just became sneakier about doing it.

Ella's hair is long, down her midback, ringlet curls. Strangers complimented her hair. Layla complimented her hair. I wanted her to hate it. I wanted her to want it straight. I wanted her to straighten it so many times that the heat would damage it. When we slept over at Layla's, I commented how it was nappy and frizzy. I told her it looked like she was wearing a wig from Grandma Judith's hair. Celebrities don't even wear their hair naturally anymore because it's ugly. Only long, straight hair, parted in the middle, slicked down to their heads, like mine, looks good. When she tried to take her time fixing, masking, and moisturizing her curls so they wouldn't be frizzy, I complained about how long she took and how much money Cara spent on the products that she needed.

I tried to get my Grandma Judith to agree that her hair was terrible and she should just give up on it. It was a lost cause. Once, while talking about how long it was taking her to put her hair up, my grandma chimed in to agree just as Ella was rounding the corner. I know she overheard it. I'm glad she did. I wanted her to learn to hate her hair. Hate the hair everyone else seemed to love, the hair I would never have.

Most of the time, I could get Layla to laugh and pick at Ella, too. On my best days, I could get Layla to help gang up on her and make her feel stupid, even if it were something trivial. We would make fun of the way she laughed, mocking her. Even more petty, we made fun of her nails. Her fingernail polish was chipped, and her nails were outgrown. Her toenails were too long, more like talons than toenails.

One day, when she was down at Layla's house, hanging out with just the two of us, we got her good. We took cans of whipped cream and started innocent enough, spraying a little dollop of cream into our mouths to eat. Rather than spraying it into her mouth, we started spraying it all over her face. It was getting into her eyes, and she was shouting for us to stop. We didn't. We started spraying it into her prized curls and smashed it in with our fingers and palms. Smeared it down her scalp. Our fingers were getting caught in her spirals as we smeared, tugged, and tore at her hair, pulling her head and neck back while the other kept spraying cream into her face and up her nose.

She was begging for us to stop and crying like a little baby. Her glasses were smeared over and knocked off. Her face and hair were ruined. Her clothes have residue of fluffy white sugar wiped all over them. She was sniffling and stuttering. I was cackling and sharing this moment of torture with Layla, bonding us even closer to one another. Ella was just a little baby, crying out for help at night.

Lillian didn't like it when we made fun of Ella. She would call me out on it, telling me to be nice to my sister. We never did anything like that in front of Lillian. Layla was in charge, but she still sought approval from her sisters. Lillian and Lauren would have been disgusted with this behavior. Never, even to their worst enemy, would they do the things I thought about doing to Ella.

When we picked at Ella, they would stand up for her when they heard us. I tried to make a big deal about the clothes she wore. She dressed like a straight dyke. She wore T-shirts and basketball shorts on the weekends. Basketball shorts that went down passed her kneecaps. Lillian said there was nothing wrong with how Ella dressed and that they wore many of the same clothes. Layla chimed in and said that Ella usually wears her clothes and asked if I thought she had ugly things. *This was not going the way I planned.* Lauren would say how jealous she is of Ella's hair and that she wished she could have long, curly hair instead of the short, thin hair she has. If anything, I could make Ella feel bad about herself, but I wasn't winning enough points with the L's. Not enough to make them discard her. Especially when I couldn't get Layla alone. She never agreed with my comments and insults when her sisters were around.

In addition to attacking her appearance, I tacked on telling the L's how dumb she was. I told them that she could barely pass math and needed extra help. I started calling her a "SPED". This really hurt Ella's feelings, but this is what happens when you try to take something that doesn't belong to you. This is what happens when you try to take my best friend. Dad chastised me, and Cara comforted Ella. As a matter of fact, Cara started giving Ella much more attention than she was giving me. She was working on extra homework and practice sheets with Ella so she would feel better about school. She reassured her that she was smart and some things are just harder for some kids than others. When Cara wasn't around, I reassured her of the opposite. I wanted her to feel stupid.

Layla didn't seem to care that Ella was struggling with math. In fact, Layla wasn't doing so great with grades in school, either. I don't think it was because she didn't understand. I think it was because she was thinking more about friends, boys, and sports and didn't want to put any effort into schoolwork.

I just wanted Layla to stop inviting Ella to join us all the time. Even when we went to the makeshift park, Ella got to come. I couldn't even tell Layla secrets without Ella overhearing. While planning my next angle, Layla and Ella chased each other around, laughing. I was infuriated. It was like Ella was flaunting Layla right before me, taunting me with my best friend. I could say I blacked out, but I didn't. I did lose all my shit, though. I just started towards her, acting like I was joining in chasing and tagging them, and then I PUSHED her straight to the ground. I stood over, shock spread across her face; Layla laughed. I laughed harder. I laughed and told her how weak she was. I pronounced how strong I was, "everyone on my mother's side of the family was such a great fighter," and I got those genes. I told her I could destroy her while she cried at my feet. I exclaimed that I could send her to the hospital if I wanted to. That's when I felt Layla's hand on my shoulder; she looked concerned. I couldn't believe what I was hearing. She wasn't congratulating me on my victory. She was telling me I was taking it too far. She looked me dead in the face with wide eyes that screamed they did NOT approve of what I was doing.

Layla pulled me to the side while Ella got herself off the ground, embarrassed, wiping tears from her flushed face. She warned me that if Ella told Cara about what I did, I was definitely going to be grounded. DAMMIT! Of course, she was right. I was going to be grounded from Layla for this, for sure. If Ella could just learn to keep her mouth shut. If she could just learn to stay out of my way. This would have never happened if she could just learn that she wasn't wanted.

We bribed her. I laughed it off and told her I was just kidding. Made her feel stupid for not being able to take a joke. Persuaded her that I never meant to push her down; I was going to fake push her but accidentally got too close. Convinced her I was playing with her and that she shouldn't tell Cara because she wouldn't understand that's how sisters play with each other. Sometimes accidents happen. I offered to buy her a few things from the store with the money I had been squirreling away. Layla convinced her mom to take us so I could make good on my offer before we had to get back home for the night. Close call.

After Ella took my bribe and promised not to tell, she told. Cara told her that no one should be putting their hands on anyone in the house. She told her hitting someone and then begging them not to tell, sister or not, is still domestic violence. She said this was no different than a boyfriend hitting you and then saying sorry and begging you not to tell the police or a family member because they were "sorry," and it wouldn't happen again.

Bitch. How dare Cara accuse me of being physically violent with my sister? Pushing her down was no big deal. So what? I taunted her. She's such a baby. She got what she deserved. She deserved to be punished. I'm not the problem. She is. She is just a snitch, baby.

I didn't get grounded from Layla, but I did get a "stern" talking from Liam. Dad and Cara didn't want to hear of me pushing Ella around anymore. Apparently, that is not how we treat sisters or children. I gave them the empty apology they were after. I'm glad she snitched, just one more thing that Layla and I can pick on her for now.

Chapter Eleven: Eyes That Pry

I'm still kind of pissed that Ella took my money and still snitched on me. I'm pissed that I got spoken to about my behavior. It's my mom's weekend now, so I decided that I was going to go after all. I want to get away from them for a while. Once I'm in the back of my Grandma Amanda's truck, I'm sulking (on purpose). I want to look disturbed so that someone will ask me what's wrong. My mom came with my grandparents to pick me up this time, which is unusual for her. She is the first to bite. I told her that I was playing with Ella, and she accidentally tripped and fell on the ground, but she lied and told everyone that I pushed her down. "What a little liar!" My mom is perturbed. She tells me that she knew Ella was going to grow up to be a "little kiss ass" and would cause problems for me. I'm relieved but slightly surprised at how easily she believed me. I keep it going and tell her that dad scolded me and threatened to push me down if he ever heard of that again. I told her Cara was calling me a liar and telling Ella to push me back next time. This even got my Grandma Amanda in a tizzy.

The whole ride to my grandma's house, everyone was chirping in and calling my dad vulgar names and telling me what a "piece of shit he has always been." My mom makes idle threats to "beat Cara's ass" for talking to her daughter like that. And me, I'm full and still feasting on the attention. I feel like, for the first time, my mom is voicing concern for me, getting defensive and angry, and being *protective* for the first time. I feel like maybe she is coming around.

We unloaded out of the truck, and my other little sister, Trudy, was waiting for me. She always seems excited to see me. She keeps badgering my mother and grandma to watch her do tricks. Any excitement I had to see her has already drifted away. She is such a nuisance. I wasn't ready to come down from the high I was getting from being the center of my mother's attention, and here Trudy came, all loud and demanding, snatching it right from my grip.

Trudy asks my mom how much longer we are staying. That's when I realized we were not staying with my grandma tonight. My mom says that Thomas is still waiting at home for us. *Who the hell is Thomas?* I give myself an exaggerated eye roll because I already know full well this is yet another boyfriend that my mother has attached herself to. She's had one that was too touchy, one that was too violent, one that was too lazy, and let me guess…this one is just right.

Thomas didn't seem too bad at first. He was skinnier than her last boyfriend. He had a crooked jaw, and his Adam's apple stuck out pretty far. He was quiet. He kind of kept to himself when we first got "home." This time, my mom found a house to live in instead of a trailer. It was small, but at least it wasn't filled to the brim with feces and dirty laundry. There were only two bedrooms, so Trudy and I were going to be bunkmates.

In the bedroom, Trudy followed me in to put my clothes from my backpack away. She said that Thomas is weird and stinks most of the time. She said he's not mean but says, "he whispers to himself a lot." I don't really think much about it. I hear people talk to themselves out loud all the time. Sometimes, when I'm alone, I talk to myself out loud, too. It makes me feel safer, like if some shadow man was going to sneak up on me, he would hear me talking out loud and think I was talking to someone else, and that would scare him away.

The next day, my mom was up before noon, another rarity for her. She tells me that she has an interview at Citgo on the corner, and my Grandma Amanda will be here to pick her up soon. I'm a little surprised that my mom is going to an interview, but I am happy for her. It's like she is really putting in some effort to be better for Trudy and me. Thomas is here, so it's not like we are going to be alone. The only other job my mom has ever had was a 2-week stent at Taco Bell. She wore a dirty purple polo shirt and smelled of sour beef. Working at the gas station will definitely be a step up from that job.

I hover over my mom while she's in the bathroom putting on makeup. I ask her about Thomas and why Trudy says he talks to himself. She says there's something different about him. He can't work because he has schizophrenia. From what I gather, that means that he sometimes hears people talking to him. She says that the doctors are trying to force him to take medicine, but he isn't sick, so he doesn't have to. She says doctors and people like Cara always try to tell people what to do, but they aren't always right. He gets the monthly check that we need, social security. She says that it's a stable source of income and enough to keep the lights on for now, but she's going to have to get a part-time job.

The conversation is cut short because we both hear my grandma's car horn at the same time. My mom is out the door, and I'm left wondering how someone gets Schizophrenia. I wonder what it's like to hear voices in your head. Are they all different voices? Or are they all the same voice? Can you have boy and girl voices? Do they only talk to you during the day and go to sleep with you at night? Or do they talk to you all night, keep you up even when you are tired, and ask them to stop?

I have many questions, but one thing is certain: there is no way I will ask Thomas. I'll just wait until tonight, and I'll try to ask my mom some of my more prying questions before bed. I'll have to think of a way to ask where she understands I am truly curious and not in a way that she thinks I am trying to be insulting.

Leftovers

Trudy and I find ourselves restless, scurrying around in the house and outside. It's raining, and we really shouldn't be running around outside and then trampling our wet shoes and boots through the house, but then again, there is no one supervising us and telling us not to. I'm in charge right now. Thomas is nowhere in sight.

He was mostly outside, sitting in the shed smoking. We pretend that we are going to avoid him and just play and mind our own business. In the end, we mostly do some snooping and spying on Thomas. When we sneak around the side of the shed, we hear him well before we catch sight of him. He is talking to himself. A lot. He's not whispering; he's talking out loud, not using an "outdoor voice," but loud enough you can make out everything he is saying even from the side of the shed.

He's having a full-blown conversation with himself. I'm pretty sure I hear him answering. *"You don't have to press start. If you press the 2 and then two 0s, it will recognize it as 2 minutes and just start the plate into rotation and begin heating it up. No, not all microwaves do that. For some of them, like most of the ones in people's houses, you have to press start still. House microwaves aren't like the hospital microwaves. Well, it doesn't matter anyway because you are not supposed to microwave the cup of noodles in the Styrofoam cup anyway. This is frustrating"!* What the heck! Who argues with themselves about microwave settings? He freaks me out.

It's a relief when my grandma's truck pulls back in. I ask her why Thomas just sits outside all day long. Why doesn't he sit inside and watch TV? My mom says being in the shed is like therapy for him. She also remarks that we can't go in the shed when he's smoking because it's not cigarettes. She smokes cigarettes in the house, but this is something stinky. I've never smelled cigarettes that smell like a rotting animal or skunk before. She says it's just a little Marijuana. She says it makes him feel better, so he doesn't need any medicine. She nudges me, so I make eye contact with her. She tells me not to tell my dad about him smoking Marijuana. She says, "It's not legal yet, but it's going to be, so it's not a big deal". I bet it makes his breath stink.

I might as well have had a visitation with this Thomas guy because my mom is leaving again. She says that it's the beginning of the month, her EBT card is reloaded, and grandma is going to take her to get some food for the house. She doesn't offer to take Trudy or me with her. Why would she when she has yet another live-in babysitter?

It was raining, but now it's more of just a sprinkle, so Trudy and I are going to go outside and run around again while it sprinkles. Thomas is still outside, sitting in one of those plastic lawn chairs. He has the radio playing next to him. He just smoking and tapping his foot to the beat of the music. We try to avoid the shed.

Trudy is getting mad because I am splashing the cold rainwater and dirt onto her when we run through the puddles. Once I see the damage I am doing, I am running around her in circles on purpose now, letting water fly up and splatter on her shirt and face. Splash by splash, she's getting soaked with water and dirt.

She is huffing like that wolf waiting to get revenge on the pigs. She yells something incoherently, and then she pushes me down. I skirt across the puddle and pebbles on the side of the house. I didn't think she had it in her. She's not scared or intimidated by me at all. My hair is now drenched with rainwater and dirt. It's cold and runs down my neck and the back of my shirt as soon as I sit up. I am fuming mad at her. She laughs and runs back to the house.

I don't even want to speak to her when I get into the house. I can't believe that little brat shoved me into a puddle. She is so unpredictable. She thinks she is in charge. I am soaking wet and cold. I just want to take a hot shower and rinse the debris out of my hair. I grabbed my oversized Nike sweats and T-shirt out of the drawer that I just put them into. I'm headed to the bathroom and tell little Miss Trudy to "leave the rest of my things" and my bag alone while I'm in the shower.

I pull back the shower curtain and find the tub is clean enough. Good. Because I didn't feel like having to clean the bathroom just to use it here. There are clean towels on the shelf, and there is VO5 green apple shampoo and conditioner sitting on the edge of the tub. I turn the knobs until I get the temperature I like and then jiggle up on the shower diverter and watch the water rainfall down.

Within a minute, I am undressed and stepping into the shower. This water is such a nice contrast to the water outside. My skin feels almost instantly clean…and warm. I rub my hands against my face several times and then run them through my hair, slicking it back onto my scalp and down my back.

The fresh scent of green apple was aerosolizing through the shower. I could feel the suds bubbling and popping in my hair. I can hear the suds fizzing and dissipating in my ears. Just as I was washing the shampoo from my hair, my body was chilled by a breeze. A breeze in a bathroom without a window…bizarre. Damn, Trudy. Probably hoping to come in a take a dump while I am relaxing and rinsing away the mud that she caused to be caked on me. I peeked out of the shower curtain, ready to chastise her, and there it was… another set of eyes staring back at me. Dark brown, emotionless, prying eyes staring straight back.

Thomas was just standing there, STARING. Staring at my naked, shriveled, and puckered skin. Staring at my stringy hair falling over the back of my shoulders. Staring at the white nail polish staining my nails, my toes curling into one another, trying to hide away from his view. Staring at my hands as I tried to shelter my prepubescent genitalia from his hollow eyes. He spoke not a word. His head was tilted just slightly to the left. His brows were furrowed, wrinkling toward his crooked nose. He didn't have a hint of a smile or a frown. His arms were dangling limp by his sides. He just stared, not even blinking.

Those minutes felt like hours. My stomach turned in knots. The voice in my head screams, "RUN RABBIT, RUN!" Any minute, the hungry wolf may devour his prey. My throat was too tight, stricken with fear, to let out an actual sound. Surely, my heart would beat right out of my chest. My fingertips were starting to get tingly, and my chest was getting tight. My head was feeling dizzy. I swear my vision wasn't blackening or narrowing; it was going white. Every hair stood up on the back of my neck. Tears welled up in my eyes by sheer terror alone, but not a single droplet spilled onto my cheeks.

Like a nightmare or a horror movie, I was experiencing flashbacks of playing house. I could already feel my skin wanting to blister up, and I hadn't even been touched. My knees were starting to wobble. I was going to give out. I couldn't bear pretending to be the mommy again. Please, not again!

He shook his head as if **I** had startled him. Then he turned his heel and walked out as quietly as he snuck in. When the knob clicked back into place, I slid down into a seated position and wrapped my arms around my legs. I let the water beat over me until it turned cold. It was like being in a dream. I felt like I was hovering over my body, watching it carry out the movements of getting out of the shower, drying off, and donning my sweatpants and worn-out t-shirt. I was moving in slow motion.

Once I made it down the hall to my room, I broke. I was bawling my eyes out. Tears ran down my face, salting my lips. I was shaking, and my breathing stuttered. I couldn't last a single second more in this house. I wanted my dad more than anything at that moment. I wanted to be safe. I wanted him to whisk me away yet again from this nightmare. My fear manifested. He didn't answer. I tried calling Cara. I left her a shaky voicemail, practically begging her to call me back. Who was going to save me now?

Crying in a fetal position on the bed was how my Grandma Amanda found me. It took everything I had to explain to her what had happened. She offered to take me to her house while my mom "sorted out" the rest. I didn't want to look at my mother as I left. I didn't want her to see me like this, broken and vulnerable. I had enough prying eyes eating away at my soul tonight. I didn't even want her pity. I just wanted to leave. To get as far away from here as possible. I swore I would never go back to that house again. That's the thing about being shackled to someone, though. No matter how terrible things are, you can be tricked into forgetting, guilted into returning, and promised that it will never be that way again.

That's what had happened right before Cara called my phone, and my grandma talked her into not coming to get me. My mother explained that it was a huge misunderstanding. She said he didn't even realize he was in the bathroom, and when he did, he immediately left. She said he was sorry. Promised this would never happen again. How could she promise me something like that? She couldn't have stopped it or prevented it. It should have never happened in the first place.

You think that you want to just go to sleep after something like that. Pretend it never happened, like you were dreaming the entire time. You don't know that sleep will be the enemy. Once I had fallen asleep, I dreamt of him. The one that stole my innocence. I never say his name. I dream of the way he groomed me into thinking that our games were innocent and normal. He groomed me to think it is okay for an adult to love a child in that manner, to kiss them on the lips "if they were in love." I dream of the way he used to wait by the front window until my mom's front tires rolled off the edge of the driveway before he started toward me.

I awoke screaming before I had to relive the way his prying eyes undressed me. Before my lips could taste the nicotine and menthol from his. Before he told me how beautiful I was. Before I felt the fat pads of his disgusting fingers slide across my cheek, tucking my hair behind my ear… I crept into my grandma's room and lay at the end of the bed on the floor, just the way you imagine the family dog would do. I curled up with a throw blanket, and the sound of my grandpa breathing nasally helped me relax enough to sleep again.

The next day didn't bring me any relief. My grandma was on her way to get my sister and mom when I woke up. My stomach felt nauseated thinking about talking to her about what happened. I ask my Pa to make me a piece of toast. Cara says when you feel sick to your stomach, you should "eat bland food."

The toast never had a chance. My mother berates me. She tells me I am overreacting and "nothing even happened." She accuses me of wanting him to want me. She says I try to ruin every relationship she's in because I am jealous.

If you don't like it at my house, then don't come back. You just cause problems anyway. Everything had been going great until I showed up. One "bad thing" happened to me, and I just can't "get over it". I'm crazy if I think she is leaving him!

Freshly cut and hemorrhaging from her words, she finishes me off with a figurative slap in the face. She's pregnant and they are going to get married, so I better get used to him. I better stop lying about him because he's going to be my new stepdad someday. "This is not the way you treat a parent"!

Grandma Amanda shouts, "That's enough"! Her fists are clenched to her sides. She storms out of the kitchen, and I scurry after her. She pulls me close to embrace me. Her chest is tremulous. I can hear her heart thudding with my face squished into her bosom. I am positive that I hear her heart rhythmically calling out, "pi-ty, pi-ty, pi-ty." I can see the ghost of my companion pity spread wickedly across her face. Even though he's invisible, I can feel pity too. He's deep in my bones, poisoning my marrow, growing a terrible tumor of mistrust and hatred. I hate her for choosing him.

Chapter Twelve: Gnawing and Numb

13 years old: Pity is the easiest means to create an ally,

then turn them against your victim.

Freshman year was not a fresh start. A "DUFF". He called me a Goddamn DUFF. For those of you thinking to yourself, what the hell is that? It's an early 2000s ridiculous insult. It's the four words that sent my freshman year into a gut-gnawing spiral. He took one look at the picture of me standing with Lauren's arms over my shoulder and, without a moment's hesitation, declared me the dumb, ugly, fat friend.

It's not just me with Lauren. It's me compared to every other single girl I know. I know I don't get the highest test scores like the goody-two-shoes, ass-kissing nerds that sit in the front, but I'm not dumb. I get decent grades. I don't have an IEP like Ella. What if people start calling me a "SPED" now? Only an actual nerd would pull out their grades to prove them wrong.

Forget being called dumb; half of the athletes have academic warnings, but coaches will never pull them from the game anyway. Their parents donate money to the school and need those players to win championships. Nobody cares about being dumb at school except the counselor and parents. It's practically cool to be dumb here. On social media, the girls with the most views are always dumb. It makes you dumber just watching their live feed.

Ugly. That word stings. I feel like the Barbie nobody ever wanted to play with. You know the one. When you go to a friend's house and you want to play with dolls. They have their favorite dolls with the best hair, makeup, and outfits. Then they have these "spare" dolls that their old aunt Kelly gave them. They don't like it as much, and they pull them out of the bottom of the bin for you to play with. It's still a doll, but you know it's just not as good as the other dolls. That's me. I feel like a wart on Layla's face. Each of the Ls is gorgeous. Not me. I'm a gross, bland potato. There is nothing special about my appearance. If anything, when I look in the mirror, I know he is right.

Ever since he called me ugly, I can't stand to look in the bathroom mirrors at school. My nose comes down into a freaky point like a damn witch. My eyebrows are too close. They would probably touch if it weren't for the tiny blue vein stuck inconveniently in the middle of my forehead. My cheeks are fluffed out. I have no lips. I am SO FREAKIN' UGLY!!! I hate myself. I hate that I look like this. I look disgusting! Why do I have to look like Amber?! Sometimes, I look impeccably the same as her when I sneer, except with teeth. Why couldn't Liam have the dominant features?

I am sobbing in the bathroom stall. I bet I look even uglier now with mascara smeared down my cheeks.

Luckily, it's not passing the time, so everyone else is in the class where I belong. I can't believe I never realized how gross I was before now. I can't believe Layla even speaks to me. I'm like a charity case friend. She will probably squeeze hanging out with the deformed-looking freak on her college resume as extracurricular activities or volunteer work. Not to mention, I'm fat.

Even now, sitting in the stall, my gut is pushed out over my jeans. I remember how much work it was this morning to get into these pants. I had to grab onto the belt loops for dear life and yank to get them on over my hips and waist. I thought it was because they were skinny jeans, but I was delusional. It's because I'm fat. If this were a confidential meeting, I would be standing up in front of a circle, introducing myself like, "Hi, I'm Ava, and I suffer from obesity."

I scroll through the selfies I have on my phone. For crying out loud, I'm fat in each one of them. I basically have a double chin. I'm so wide. I thought I just had a larger bone structure. I'm not even sure if that is a real thing now. My arms look like an English teacher who gave up on herself after her divorce. My torso is a refrigerator box. The worst part is I have all this fat and no actual curves. I don't have a gap between my thighs like Layla. I don't have the buns of a baseball player. I don't even have boobs. I just have little spuds that sprouted in their place on my lumpy potato body.

I feel like my clothes are cutting into my sides by the time I get up and leave the stall. I'm headed to the health aid. I'm going to tell her I have really bad period cramps so that I can go home. I can't think about anything else right now. I feel like, rather than a poorly delivered insult, I have been drenched in some sort of oily film. I wish I could just wash away this disturbing fat shell off me. I don't want anyone else to see me today. I can't help but wonder how many people have known this about me but have been too nice to say something to my face. No wonder Layla always has guys texting her and asking her out. Not a single guy even looks my way. Now I know why. I'm a blubbery little DUFF.

I am brooding in my bed. I'm disappointed like finding out Santa isn't real. This person, the body I thought I had been living in, was fictitious. I am the fat man behind the curtain. I would rather be numb than feel this way. I have the lights off because I don't want to accidentally see my reflection on my full-length mirror hanging on the side of my closet. I can't believe this is happening to me. There's a little voice in the back of my head that tells me this is payback for being so nasty to Ella. When Cara knocks on my door and tells me dinner is ready, I tell her I feel sick (and I do mentally) and don't think that I can eat dinner.

That split second did it for me. I was going to starve myself. I would lose weight if I never ate anything. Models do it all the time, right? I feel like I heard some days they eat nothing but a single grape. I can't bear another day in my Proboscis monkey body. Something has to give. And right now, I have to give up eating.

Dinner time came and went. Easy peasy. I need to do some research on how to go about starving myself. I know that I have to eat something, but I need to know how many calories the bare minimum I need to consume in one day. I pulled open my laptop and typed into the Bing search engine "How to starve yourself". Talk about negative. Every site keeps reiterating how unhealthy it is to starve yourself. "It's a form of self-harm." I don't want to be healthy; I want to be skinny. The only helpful site tells me some experts believe the body can survive a couple of months without food. I don't plan not to eat at all; I just plan to eat as little as possible.

Starving takes willpower. It is not for the weak. You don't realize all of society revolves around consuming food until you purposely avoid it. The first few days are the worst. After about five days, it started to get easier. I stopped going to breakfast at school. I had to go to lunch but stopped getting my own tray. If people asked about it at the table, I just told them everything looked disgusting. Everyone knows school lunch is the worst. The smell of food made me salivate. I would salivate so much it would nauseate me.

Leftovers

In about three weeks, I had already lost 8 pounds. My jeans slid over my hips much easier. To be honest, I could barely think about eating. It took every ounce of energy to even get out of bed. I am so fatigued. All I want to do is sleep. My dad thinks I am depressed, and I want him to think that. It's better than him knowing the truth. He keeps trying to talk to me, to cheer me up. I had to give him something, so I told him that a boy was being mean to me and told me I was ugly. Liam tells me that I am beautiful and that boys are just punks and not to let it bother me. I leave out the rest. I don't want to bring up anything about weight because I know that will draw his attention to what I am secretly achieving. I tell him I am embarrassed and beg him not to talk to Cara about it.

After six weeks, I am down at total of 15 pounds. I have daily headaches and body aches. I have only enough energy to go to school and come back. Period. I have to stay under my covers at all times. I am so cold; it's like I am already dead. I have mastered getting through the nausea by only consuming low-calorie bread that Cara just happens to buy already. I toast it with nothing else. I also have a stash of Saltine crackers on my bedside. They give me a few calories but also help to settle my stomach temporarily. The gnawing sensation is the worst thing I have ever had to endure. It never goes away. It's like a cat is constantly kneading my insides with its claws.

Initially, I struggled to be around food, but that is in the past.

To appease Liam and keep this masquerade of invented depression up, I come down long enough to make a plate and then head back up to "eat in my room." Really, I just throw the whole plate into my waste can. When we go out, I try to shuffle my food around on the plate to make it appear that I have eaten. I pretend that I like cold fries better so I am not expected to eat them at the table and can get a to-go box. If I must eat something in front of them, I will only eat one chicken tender and then complain about the taste or two chicken wings instead of the 8 I ordered. Liam hassles Ella when she doesn't eat the food she's ordered. Tells her she's being wasteful. He doesn't say a thing when I do it. Probably worried I'm too sensitive and will just start crying at the table or something.

By week 8, I have lost a total of 20 pounds. I am so proud of myself for sticking with it. By week 10, I have hit a plateau. I didn't lose a single pound this week or last. I don't understand. I read that cranberry juice could make you "have a flat stomach in just two weeks." I've been chugging that bitter liquid by the jug and haven't seen any results. I have a little food baby. I am so bloated. I haven't pooped in days. It is so hard to get anything out. I have to strain and sweat even to get pebbles pushed out. Being a teenage girl, I could blame the lack of weight loss and bloat on my period, except I haven't had one in the last two months.

I already feel like complete dog shit when Liam comes up to my room and lays it out for me. He says Cara has been irritating him that she is concerned about me, practically harassing him about me. Apparently, she noticed my school lunch account hadn't been charged and has been tracking that behind my back for several weeks now. She has been accusing me of starving myself to him. He said at first, he didn't believe her, but then again, he noticed I had lost a lot of weight in the last two months.

I was going to lie straight to his face. Tell him his beloved little wife was just picking on me until he pulled out his phone. That bitch had been coming into my room while I was at school and was taking photos of the food I had been dumping to prove to Liam that I was lying about eating this entire time.

While crying, I tell him it's her fault I have been starving myself. She is always bragging about how skinny she is. She had just commented the other day that she was the lightest person in the whole house to Liam. I know that comment was made towards me. She just wants me to be fat.

She practically called me obese. I tell him she is always making sneaky comments about my weight. She told me and Ella that we couldn't eat all the chips and snacks in one day because if we made a habit out of it, we would grow up and be obese. When we were arguing, after I had hit Ella again down at the Ls house and she snitched me out again, Cara said I couldn't just go around beating up a child just "because I'm bigger than her." I know she meant fat when she said bigger. I told him she has been purposefully buying me size medium clothes when I wear small just to rub it in my face that she thinks I am fat. He doesn't know what to say. He just sits there, looking sorry, feeling pity for me.

***

Everything has to be a charade in this house. Of course, Liam told Cara what I told him in private. And, of course, she told him I was just upset because I got caught. Cara printed out an article about the consequences of starvation. Just because she works in the medical field, she thinks you should always have evidence to support your opinions. I don't need her fucking article. I already know that starvation is bad. Bing told me that the very first night, I started googling it. She told me I was already displaying all of the adverse effects of starvation: extreme fatigue, cold intolerance, constipation, changes in menstruation, and dry skin/scalp, and she was worried about me. She said she started putting everything together after I missed my periods and asked her for dandruff shampoo. I had severe abdominal pain one day from the awful gnawing and asked to stay home. By then, she had already learned about me not eating at school. I should have known she was getting suspicious when she asked me that day when the last time I ate something was. You don't really think clearly when you are basically dying, though. She told me I have to start eating, that this isn't the way. She told me I would lose my teeth next if I kept it up.

I hate when she is right and rubs it in your face. I cannot afford to lose my teeth. This has me scared. No matter how skinny I can get, no guy is going to be interested in me without teeth. My mother doesn't have most of her teeth. I cannot look like my mother. Screw Cara.

She only noticed because she hates me. She thinks I am just like my mom, and she is always waiting for me to make mistakes. She's always picking on me. She just wants my dad to think Ella is better than me. She thinks she is better than me. She's probably glad I got caught starving myself so she can just make fun of me. She probably hopes I will never get as skinny as Layla and Lauren. She wants me to be the DUFF. Maybe she should learn to mind her own Goddamn business.

When you get caught lying, it makes you feel angry. Worse than that is when you are accused of things you aren't doing. I've been practicing anorexia, not bulimia. I never puke after I eat. I can't stand to vomit. Cara gives me the side eye whenever I get up to go to the bathroom while we are out for dinner. By the third time getting up, she asks what I'm doing in there. She says I never get up thrice in one hour to use the restroom at home. I can tell she's suspicious and even sent Ella into the restroom once to check on me. I'm not purging my food. I can tell other people in the family are starting to wonder the same thing. Why does she have to embarrass me? Would she feel better if she knew I wasn't purging? I was just stalking boys on social media. Making fun of fat girls in our class with Layla rather than sitting at the table with them; disappointment in their eyes.

When you are in the mood for a pity party, call Judith. She despises Cara. She took away her first-born son like Rumpelstiltskin. Cara doesn't take shit from Judith and tells her she needs to have more respect and boundaries. Cara tells her that she favors me and treats Zack like he doesn't exist. Cara is sick of Judith. Judith is easy to manipulate. Cara is not wrong. Judith all but grovels at my feet. I feel like I am filling a void for her. She needs to be loved and wanted. Now that my dad has Cara, he doesn't need Judith anymore. Cara surely doesn't need or want Judith. My grandpa John is always busy working. He barely gives her any attention. I'm the daughter she wished she had kept. When you despise someone, you instantly believe everything bad you hear about them. That's how easy it was to make Judith hate Cara. Filling Judith's head with horror stories and making Cara out to be the evil stepmother and me, the helpless victim, was too easy.

If Liam weren't going to take my side, then Judith would. She cringed when I fabricated story after story about how awful Cara was. Talking with Judith was like a substitution for talking with my own mother. They both detested Cara, so they didn't mind adding on and agreeing with every single word I sold them. Judith wasn't like a grandma to me at all. She acted like a toxic teenager. She gossiped and kept secrets for me. I made her promise not to tell Liam. I told her that telling him would only make things worse for me, because he never believed me and would just take Cara's side. I was such an outsider in their home. I felt like I didn't belong there. She coddled me and told me, "I would always have her." She would never call me a liar like Liam.

I didn't stop with Judith. I started telling stories about Cara to basically anyone who would listen. I told stories about how she victimized me all the time to the L's. I told them elaborate stories about how mean she was. She was certifiably crazy. She had the most extreme mood swings. I never knew which Cara I was going to get when I came home. I had to walk on eggshells around her. I told them that she gave me all the worst chores. She would punish me if I didn't do them to her satisfaction. She was knit-picking everything I did and didn't do. I told them that Liam would just stand back and watch her belittle me and tell me how ugly, in fact, I was. Whenever Ella tried to step in and tell them that I was lying, I would lash out and call her a mama's girl. Layla and I would take turns making fun of her. I would push her around and say that she's always just trying to stand up for her little mommy.

Something had come over me. I truly felt like Cara needed to pay. She deserved this for sneaking around my back. My room is my private space, and she had no business going through my things, even if it was just my trash. I don't want to hear it was with good intentions. She deserves to pay for telling my father I was a liar. Leading others to believe I was purging my food. LIES! No one cares about her opinions. Leave that bullshit about healthy goals and proper ways to lose weight for her patients. Just because she went back to school and got a new degree, she thinks she knows every fucking thing. I don't want to hear that she is worried about me because she loves me. She doesn't care about me. *She's the worst wolf of them all, the leader of the pack.* No one cares about me.

Chapter Thirteen: Baddies Make Their Own Rules

Don't clear the path. Step on heads to get what you want.

Now that I have starved myself skinny, I am halfway to my goal. I want to be an "it" girl. I want to believe the DUFF in me has died, and I am replacing her with a hot girl exterior. This is when I decided that being friends with Layla wasn't enough. I need to become Layla. I will style my hair like her hair. I will wear my makeup (actually, I will wear her makeup) the way she does. I will get my nails done just like she does: medium-length, coffin-shaped, all-white gel polish. White nail polish means you are single and looking. I will wear gold hoop earrings. At school, everyone knows that the bigger the hoop, the more scandalous things you are willing to do with a guy.

I'm going to wear nothing but cropped tops to show off my newly skinny waist. I am a late bloomer and haven't developed much breast yet, so I'll just see if I can sneak some of Layla's padded bras, or I could always use the cotton pads I wash my face with to stuff my bra instead.

I can't continue to starve myself since I have been caught completely. Liam and Cara are keeping a better eye on my eating habits now. I can't pretend to eat in my room any longer. I have to sit at the dinner table with the rest of the family. I have slowly started eating again and I have to admit I do feel better. I can get out of bed without the agony of needing to get back into it. Cara took the scale out of the bathroom. She says I was becoming obsessed with weighing myself and was developing an unhealthy self-image. I'll just weigh myself in the locker room at school or first thing in the morning before we leave for Layla's house.

Layla has perfectly blonde hair. I want to dye my hair blond. Surprisingly, Grandma Judith doesn't jump right on board with this idea. I tried to get her to dye my hair when I went to her house behind dad and Cara's back. She said that it would damage my hair. I like my hair, but she loves it. She tells me how long it is getting and doesn't want me to ruin it. She says I should just get highlights if I have to color it. I've seen her do highlights before. Not good. Chunky and yellow instead of blonde. She's not really a cosmetologist, just a barber. She fawns over my hair for the rest of the night, and I am convinced to leave it this way.

My dad actually pisses me off. He won't let me get any "revealing" clothing. He says I am too young and crop tops are not appropriate for my age group. He says there are a lot of perverts out there, and he doesn't think I should dress that way. He tried the whole "if a guy doesn't like you unless you are dressed like that, he's not the guy for you" speech on me. If I ask my grandma

Amanda or mom to buy the clothes, they will do it. My mom will buy them just to spite Liam. Until I can get them ordered, I'll just sneak around and wear Layla's tops. I have taken some of my old shirts that don't fit and started tucking and rolling them to make crop tops out of those ones, too.

I start talking more flirtatiously. I want guys to overhear me saying provocative things so they will be interested in me. I used to tell Cara stories about the girls that dressed this way. I told her how disgusting it was that girls were trying to take other girls' boyfriends. It was repulsive that girls were sleeping around at school already. Some even got an infection, Chlamydia. One girl messed up and found herself pregnant. She was a grade higher than me, a sophomore. She didn't care about anything, scrappy. She got into a fistfight and had to go to juvie pregnant. Those are the girls that get asked on dates, though. Girls like me, DUFFs, never get asked out. We don't even get asked if we have a spare pen or piece of gum. If listening to trashy rap, wearing skintight clothing, and wearing hoops that touch my shoulders is what it takes, then that is what I will make happen.

Everything about my demeanor has changed. I squeeze sexual innuendo into every conversation. I want to sound experienced. It's not just my clothes. I have started copying the way influencers speak. I mimic phrases they use. Any opportunity I get to prove I'm "a baddie," I do it. All the It girls at the school can't be bothered to be there. I found myself skipping class in the bathrooms. Not even because I really wanted to, but because some of the older classmen were doing it and asked if I was skipping. I didn't want to look like a loser, so I said yes and stayed in there, propping myself against the wall. I even skipped and snuck over to the football field and was hanging out on the bleachers with my new *friends* when we got caught and hauled back to the high school.

I have been trying to complete challenges from social media to gain popularity. Layla is becoming more mischievous and rebellious. Just like a shadow, I follow suit. Anything she suggests, we do it. We were stealing stuff from the school for challenges. Stealing things from the church. We even stole a sign from our neighbor's yard and ran across the wooded lot to hide it. He caught us on his ring doorbell camera and threatened to call the cops if we didn't put it back exactly where we found it. I dumped out some food into our neighbor's driveway. Layla doesn't like this neighbor's mom. She wrote her a vulgar and abrasive letter and put it in her mailbox. She wrote that she was a shitty parent and a whore. I do not have the guts or balls, your pick, to do that, so I stuck to the littering. Even that I had a hard time getting away with it, she called us right out on it and demanded it get picked up immediately. I tried to blame it on Ella and then begged her to pick it up because I was "too embarrassed" to pick it up myself.

I had my first nasty rumor going around. Some kid was going

around telling everyone that the day I skipped at the football field, I was sucking his dick under the bleachers. He told my cousin about this. It was going around the middle school about what a nasty tramp I was becoming. I wanted attention, but I felt dirty. I wanted guys to think about me sexually, but when I heard the rumors out loud, I felt cheap and sick. It made me wonder if there was a girl sitting at her kitchen table with her mom, telling her stories about the nasty girl at school, me being that nasty girl.

Down at Layla's house, we talk about boys all the time. Layla is boy-crazy. We talk about all the boys we have a crush on. Layla pushed to see how far I would go with them. I tell her I want to do sexual things because I know that's what she wants to hear. That's what anyone at school wants to hear or talk about now. We talk about getting older and getting sugar daddies to take care of us. That's what all-grown men want anyway, right? Young, sexy girls like us hanging on their arms, we might as well get something out of the deal. I feel like everywhere I go now, I catch men staring at me. They want to be with me. I feel like when her uncle comes over now, he is always staring at me. He looks me over like a treat he just wants to sink his sweet tooth into. He's never spoken to me, playing hard to get, I guess. I want him to flirt with me.

While the four of us were jumping on Layla's trampoline, Layla, Ella, Lillian, and me, apparently, some creepy old guy, was watching us in his truck parked in our cul-de-sac. He had the nerve to approach Layla's mom and tell her that he had been watching us from his truck and he liked what he'd seen. He said he liked the small blonde one the best, Layla (ugh, of course, he liked Layla better than me). She freaked out and chased him off. She told her husband, and he spoke with the other dads in the neighborhood. If this were a movie, they would have peeled out in a truck and hunted him down, probably buried him in an isolated area, and then made a secret pact to never talk about it again.

After that, we were all worked up in Layla's room. Talking about what ifs. What if you were kidnapped? What if they tried to grab just one of us? What if he tried to rape you? I wanted to be nonchalant. Like it wouldn't bother me, and I wasn't scared. I told the group I would fight him. If he still captured me, it wouldn't be so bad anyway. It wouldn't matter if he raped me. "Round 2, I guess". That silenced the room. Then I laughed. For the first time, I told them the Spark Notes version of my childhood "incident." Then I laughed out loud again. Like, so what? I'm damaged. Ha Ha Ha.

***

Anyone who is anyone vapes. Layla wanted to start vaping, so we found a girl who gets them from her older brother, Jocelyn, and we started trying them. They taste delicious. You can get them in so many flavors: cotton candy, bubble gum, blue raspberry, etc. I'm not sure how I am supposed to feel after I hit the vape, so I just act whatever way Layla does. We didn't want to get caught or snitched on, so we invited Ella over and then pushed her into vaping, too. We literally shoved it in her face even after she said no. Jocelyn scratched it against her lips and pressed it into her teeth until she just gave in and took a hit. Her lips were bleeding while she took her first puff. Layla started to feel bad about it and said we shouldn't make her if she really doesn't want to do it. We've come this far, though. It's part of the plan. The smart part is I have Ella keep the vape on her person. If our parents find it, Ella will take the fall, not me.

I used to be a good kid. I followed the rules. I did what was expected of me. Cara expects after school that you complete your homework and then your daily assigned chore and then you get to have the rest of your night for leisure. I decided a baddie wouldn't be following those kinds of rules. Besides, my mom says I don't have to listen to Cara. She's not my mom. She doesn't get to decide what I do with my time. I don't bother spending any time on my homework. And I absolutely do not do my chores. From now on, I'll decide what I want to do with my time.

A few months have passed, and things at home are heating up. Ella got caught with the vape. She bent over to pick up her shoes, the vape slipped right out of her shirt in front of my dad. She is not a ride-or-die chick. She threw me directly under the bus. She told the entire story of where we got it and who was all using it. I tried to convince Liam that she was lying and the vape was hers only. I told him that I tried it a few times but didn't like it. She kept on doing it anyway. He wasn't buying that story. That snake of a woman, Cara, took it upon herself to text Layla's dad and tell him about the vape. She ended up getting caught with another one in her room and grounded.

Dad found out that my grades were slipping because of all my missing assignments. He said this was not something that would be tolerated in this house and told me that I would be grounded until my grades came back up. I bet he only found out about my grades because of Cara. That nosey bitch was probably checking my grades online. How I'm doing in school is none of her business. She's not my mom. No matter how hard she tries, she'll never be my mom. I have one. My mom says that I should continue to let my grades drop. She says that that will show Liam that he cannot control me.

I came home one day, went straight to my room, and found my clothes folded at the end of my bed. Cara must have done my laundry. Now that I've decided I'm not doing any chores, my clothes are always overflowing out of my basket. When I start sifting through them, I realize I'm missing all of Layla's crop tops I've been borrowing and sneaking under my sweaters until I get to school. Those clothes do not belong to her. She does not have the right to take Layla's things from me. I am fuming pissed.

I tell my mom that Cara has been snooping through my things and stealing my clothes. I tell her she just thinks I'm fat, and that's why she won't let me wear the crop tops. My mom shares a few choice words to call Cara.

If she has to keep hearing about Cara insulting me and stealing from my room, she's going to beat Cara's ass. She has no authority over me, and it's not up to Cara to decide what I am allowed to wear. Cara is jealous of my body and wishes she looked like me; she wishes she was young and sexy. She's just jealous because she never looked this good. Why does she care about how I dress? Cara was a whore when she was younger. Didn't she have Zack at 17 years old? Who the hell is she to go around judging and restricting me?

My mom says not to worry about the clothes. She'll have my Pa buy me new clothes to replace those ones. What I'm worried about is what I'm going to tell Layla when she asks for her clothes back.

My mom tells me she would just buy them, except she's living at my Grandma Amanda's house again. She has to use all of her money for the new baby. The food stamps increased, and she was able to get WIC again, but she still had to buy diapers, and this little guy is a big pooper. Thomas went batshit crazy when he found the messages on my mom's phone between her and her last boyfriend. She said after she had my brother, she felt lonely and didn't feel like Thomas loved her anymore or found her attractive. She had been sneaking behind his back, cheating with Kyle. She tells me Kyle was a better lover than Thomas. I cringe when she says those words. That is not something I like to imagine my parents doing, making love. She said maybe he should have been taking his meds after all.

A pattern would have it: he also came to the same fork in the road every man before crossed. He didn't want her. He was not going to put up with her using him and cheating on him. He called her a worthless pig bitch whore and stormed out of the house. Needless to say, after he set the porch ablaze, with her and both of my siblings asleep in the early morning hours, he never came back to the house again. He was picked up and taken to the hospital. He needed acute care to stabilize his Schizophrenia, and then he was going to jail. I can't say I'm sad to hear it. Now, I never had to worry about playing house with him. Without his social security, though, Mom couldn't even make the subsidized housing payment and had to tuck her tail between her legs and head back to Grandma Amanda's house.

I called Judith and stirred up the same shit. I tell her it's hard to live in a house that is so strict. I cannot be myself, my true self, in this house. I tell her that the only way I will keep friends or look pretty is if I wear those clothes. All of the popular kids wear skimpy clothes; if I don't, I'm a freak. I tell her Cara does not want me to be popular or beautiful. She wants me to be second-rate to Ella. If Ella wasn't so self-conscious about her body, I bet Cara would let her wear these clothes. Judith agrees with me. It doesn't matter if this is Cara's house or not. It is my room, and she has no right to be in my room. I love getting Judith all riled up.

Before my dad gets home from work, I call and leave him a message, too. I was just letting him know that his bitch of a wife took it upon herself to go in my room and take my things. Adding a small lie to ignite the flames, I tell him that other clothes have gone missing, too. I tell him that she has also taken jeans that belonged to Lillian, and she's been asking for them back, but I can't find them. I know that Cara took them! I want Liam to be bombarded with this. I beg Judith to call and talk to him. Not about everything. Just this. I want her to persuade him that Cara is the problem. She needs to respect my privacy, and he needs to take her parental authority away.

Judith tells him that Cara is just the stepparent and she really shouldn't be making decisions for me. She says that she used to dress in crop tops when she was younger, which is not a big deal. She presses him for me. She pushes that this will help me to be happier. It's like she has a pullstring on her back, and I have pre-recorded all of the sayings.

"It makes her feel pretty. She just wants to fit in. She is depressed, and this is the only way to make things better for her. All her friends are wearing these clothes; why does he want me to stand out in a bad way? A little skin showing never hurt anyone".

Liam is confused, and why wouldn't he be? He's being pulled in a million directions, I would know. I am the one yanking most of the strings. He should be able to trust his mother's advice, right? He had a stepfather growing up, and he knows how it feels to be treated like an ugly duckling. When a child confides in you and says they are having a problem, you are supposed to take it at face value and believe everything they say, right? Why would a child make something like this up? Obviously, Cara is the problem. She is harassing me.

Cara admits that she took the clothes. They have talked about this several times before, and she expects Liam to hold up to his side of their partnership. He can't just go around changing the rules just because I don't like them. He can't just decide to undermine her just because a thirteen-year-old wants him to. My mom sure as shit doesn't want Cara to have any say in what I do, say, or dress like. She even left him a voicemail saying he better tell Cara to straighten up or "the black Sheba is going to get her ass."

No matter what decision he makes, he'll be the bad guy. I want so badly for him to choose me. She deserves to fall. I made

Zack fall from his pedestal before, and I am ready to shove her straight over a cliff. After a long-heated argument in the basement, I so desperately strained my ear to try to hear; Liam says the rule will stick. No crop tops. He says they made the decision together, but I know he is a liar. Cara made the decision, and he's too scared to disobey her. He's like a dog. He does whatever tricks she tells him to as long as she offers him a treat at the end of the day. I hate him. I tell him this. I tell him that he's a hypocrite. He talks about how sad he is that my mom never chose me, but he does the same thing. He always takes Cara's side, not mine. I beg him to divorce her. We could be so happy together, just me and him. We don't even have to take Ella. She's just like her mom anyway. I hate her, too. I hate her personality. She's such a snitch.

I'm dizzy from spiraling in my head. Nothing ever goes my way. I read myself affirmations every morning about how I don't run; I attract. *"I'm admired by everyone who crosses my path. Everything I desire comes to me effortlessly. There's no struggle in my story. My aura radiates love and beauty. I deserve to have my desires granted to me. I have so much love for myself. I don't chase, I attract. I am powerful and attract love into my life easily and effortlessly".* I need to do something drastic. I need to send her a message. I am in charge, not her.

As though my energy manifested the opportunity for me, it fell into my lap. Unbeknownst to Dad and Cara, I had been sneaking around and vaping here and there. I even indulged in my first joint hanging out with Layla and Jocelyn. Layla, being Layla, was not a one-woman show. Just because Jocelyn could get her vape and the occasional weed from her grandfather's cabinet, Layla had been spending much more time with Jocelyn. She would make plans with me and then cancel at the last minute. I would see on her social media feed that she was hanging out with Jocelyn instead.

I confronted Layla and told her that she had to choose between Jocelyn and me. I implied that if she chose Jocelyn, I would have Ella tell Cara about the marijuana. Cara was sure to tell her dad. Blackmail works every time. Layla chose me. Somehow, Jocelyn had found out that I was behind Layla not wanting to hang out with her anymore. Jocelyn lived with her grandparents because her parents couldn't care for her. She had a mean streak and was more of a rebel than Layla and I combined. To get back at me, she snuck over to our house, hood covering her face, and pulled up a video we had made of me vaping (luckily, not of me sucking on the end of a joint) and played the digital masterpiece to be recorded by our doorbell camera.

That little gesture meant war. Layla got me all pumped up. Said I should beat her up. I had never actually fought before. I had talked a big game to Ella and made some wild-ass threats, but inside…chicken shit. Layla said it was time for Jocelyn to go down, and I had to beat her up. I had to prove to Layla that she had chosen

the right friend. Joceyln was in middle school. I was a freakin'
freshman for crying out loud. I was going to do it. Not only that, but
I was going to have Layla film it. Then we would spread it around
the entire school so everyone knew what a weak piece of shit
Jocelyn was, and I could earn the status I had been striving for. She
would think twice before messing with me again.

Layla stirred the pot and got Jocelyn to agree to fight me.
She lived just around the road from me, so we were going to meet
at the small Seventh-Day Adventist church and fight near the
playground. I brought Layla, but because she couldn't keep her big
mouth shut, Ella tagged along, too. The fight went down alright. It
was over before I knew it. My legs were trembling, and my heart
was working overtime in my chest. I was terrified to be face-to-face
with Jocelyn. Somehow, I've forgotten how big she was. I was
hoping that she was scared, too. Layla had her phone out, ready to
direct a fight worthy of pay-per-view. I started screaming at Jocelyn
to hit me. I thought by telling her to throw the first swing, she would
be too scared to do it. The fight would dissipate and really become
us throwing insults back and forth at one another. I was wrong.

She struck me straight in my face. Nailed me in my left
orbital. I saw instant stars. After that, I could barely see out of the
tears welling up in my eyes. I had never been hit like that before. It
wasn't over after the first strike. She kept nailing me in my head,
swing after swing. It was like she was hammer-fisting my scalp. I

tried windmilling my arms to make contact with her. Even when my fist did, by mere chance alone, connect with her, all of the force behind it had already dissolved. She'd thrown me on the ground. I busted my right hip, eating up the fall. My knee rocked in the wrong direction. I tried hitting her in the stomach while, at the same time, trying to push my legs up to get me on my feet again. She damn near ripped my shirt off. The cotton smeared across my eyes, drying my tears but still leaving me blind. She entangled my hair between her fingers and yanked me around. She was tuckered out, and I could tell she didn't want to fight anymore. She wasn't in the best shape. I finally managed to scrape my body from the lawn, and as she was turning away to leave, my knuckles chaffed against the tip of her nose. That was it. Fight over.

Layla had already pressed send, lighting up Ella's phone for a video received. We reviewed the video in the privacy of Layla's room. This turned out to be more of a small viewing for the audience of her sisters, whom she had already messaged. I looked ridiculous being tossed around like a damn rag doll. I felt the heat in my face now, but seeing the instantaneous black eye form after her first punch was mind-blowing. It looked like she'd hit me so hard my neck could have snapped. I definitely didn't want this video going around the school.

I could tell Layla was sensing my disappointment about how the fight had turned out, even though her own adrenaline was still pumping. She started making comments about the "good swings" I had thrown. She said she got lucky with that sucker punch. In reality, though, she didn't sucker punch me. I saw that white-knuckled fist coming straight at my face. I was just too stunned to move, to block the punch. I liked Layla's version better, though. So, that is the version I plan to stick with. From landing on the ground, my knuckles got scraped, and there were speckles of dried blood across my hands and fingers. In the video, after Jocelyn turned to leave, I realized she never turned around again in the video. I insert my own victory here. I tell everyone that I bloodied her nose at the end. I show them the blood on my hand and tell them it is from her nose. They cheered me on and let me bask in my fictitious win.

When Cara pulled up from work just an hour later, I knew I was going to be in trouble. Ella had already ratted me out to Liam. Oh, and let me tell you, Cara was hot.

What the hell goes on when I'm not home? What were you thinking? What has gotten into you? What part of that little mind of yours decided that was a good idea? And you dragged your sister along for the show. You have been so disappointing lately. First, you were sneaking around vaping. Then you coerce your little sister to do the same. You have been fat-shaming her every time you think no one can hear you. You've been skipping class. You've been getting bad grades. You've been stealing. You've been sneaking around our backs, taking pictures, and posting them of yourself dressed in those

Goddamn crop tops. You have trashy rumors circling about you. What were you thinking? You can't get away with hitting Ella anymore, so now you have to try beating up other people instead. Does this make you feel good about yourself? You are on the wrong path. If you don't straighten up, you're going to end up in juvie or worse. You should be ashamed of yourself preying on children to make yourself look cooler.

After that reaction, Dad said I was grounded from Layla. She was a bad influence on me; I should have known better. I don't know which was worse, being yelled at or hearing that I was such a disappointment. I already had to go to school the next day with a black eye. I feel like that would be punishment enough. Seeing how punishments were being doled out, I was getting ready to serve Cara hers.

Chapter Fourteen: Bad Intentions

Even the Nicest People have their Limits

The next morning, I got up for school with bad intentions. I pulled out a cropped shirt I had been hiding inside my pillowcase so that Cara wouldn't find it. I slipped it on and went downstairs, pretending to eat breakfast, with the hopes that Cara would see me in the shirt. She came shuffling down the steps to let the dogs outside, and she noticed right away. She firmly advised me that I would not be wearing that shirt today and instructed me to change. But today…today, I was not going to change it. I went about my routine and finished readying myself. As part of my punishment, I could not ride with Layla to school. I was going to have to hitch a ride with Cara before she went to work this morning. I was getting anxious the closer the clock reached time to leave. I headed downstairs, proudly displaying my stomach in the top she requested I change out of.

When she saw the shirt, everyone in the room could hear her taking a long sigh to herself, trying to contain her anger. She looked me straight in the black eye and told me, "Today is not the day," and she was not going to tell me nicely again to change that shirt so we could leave. "NO!" I said it with every amount of bravery I had in me. With gritted teeth, she warned me not to press her today. I boldly told her to go wake my dad up because I was not changing. "He'll just take my side anyway." Pleasantries aside, she forcefully told me to get my ass up those stairs and change that fucking shirt. By the look in her eye, I could tell if I didn't get up the stairs, she would rip that thing right off of me. She was at the edge. She just needed a push.

I stomped up the first few steps, and I could hear her telling Ella to head out to the car. I swung my head around, scowling. I told her she was going to be out there waiting for a while because I was going to take my damn time. She ran her hand over her chin and down her neck, forcing the anger to push back down. I could hear her following up the steps when my feet hit the landing upstairs. I rushed to my room. I hadn't made a real decision on my next move. I took the crop top off and grabbed a hoodie from the floor. I could hear her in the hall, waiting. Not even bothering to whisper, I said, "You are such a bitch!" Before I could try to register whether she had heard the words intended for her, my door swung open. She was there over the edge. And I was the one to push her.

"Oh, I'm a bitch now? Grab your shit and let's get going". It wasn't even my voice anymore, just a trembling replica. "Well, you're acting like a bitch". Without even a single pause for hesitation, she replied, "Well, you're acting like a cunt, so grab your shit and get your ass down those stairs." I grasped my hoodie close to me. I had made up hundreds of stories villainizing her. I had a million fake scenarios in my head where I said all kinds of things that would have made my mother proud, but that word was from her lips. It was worse than anything I had ever experienced. Worse than anything, I had made up about her. She had never actually spoken to me with that kind of venom on her tongue. I was truly shocked and heartbroken all at the same time.

She had gone downstairs to cool down and wait for me in the car. I thought this was what I wanted. I wanted her to be the villain. Now, I had a real reason to call her a monster, and I wished I had never heard it. I had once overheard her say to be careful in relationships because all the scars on her heart were from people who had told her they loved her. This hurt I felt now would never heal. I had repeatedly forgiven Amber; that is how a trauma bond works. But this scar, this scar would keloid up. I was walking through my thoughts, feet like molasses, before I realized I was standing in the kitchen staring into the fridge.

Cara came through the front door about the same time I was coming back to my senses. She asked what the hell I was doing. Then she announced she had had enough. She told me to give her my phone. Every part of my reasonable brain was screaming to hand it over to her. But the only voice I was listening to now was my mother's. *Don't give her that phone. She has no authority over you. She has no right to take your things. Just wait until your dad hears what she called you. Her reign is over.*

I clenched that phone like it was the very edge of the cliff I had just pushed her off. I wasn't giving her my phone. She started toward me, and for no real reason, I thought, this is it. This is where she beats the sense right back into me (she had never, not even once, spanked me as a child). I started screaming, "Get away from me, don't touch me"! She snatched that phone from my hand so fast that the air around us didn't even have time to react. "Out!" was all she demanded, fingers shooting toward the door. This time, I obeyed.

As you would have expected, I cried wolf to every single person that was willing to listen. At school, for one moment, I even thought about lying and telling people Cara had given me this black eye, but by then, Layla had already shared the story about mine and Jocelyn's fight. It would be an easily detected lie and would make me look like more of a fool.

By the time I talked to my mom, Cara had basically ripped the shirt off me upstairs. She called me a cunt...and I, of course, hadn't said anything to her to provoke such a horrifying name to call a child. She had grabbed me by the arm, pinching it until I finally let go of the phone. She tormented me on the way to school (the car was eerily quiet on the ride to school this morning). My mom could have come through the phone right then and there.

By the time I called Judith, she had already heard an even more elaborate version from my mom and Grandma Amanda. I hadn't even bothered objecting to anything they fostered up in their minds. Judith was pacing. She couldn't believe what a step monster Cara had become. She was getting out of control. Judith was offering to let me live with her by the end of that call. She would convince Liam to get me out of that environment. It was too emotionally damaging for such a sweet grandchild to endure.

I was just a child by the time Liam found out about the morning's events. An innocent victim. Cara was on an impulsive rampage. According to Judith, it didn't even matter what I had or hadn't done; calling an innocent child a cunt was unforgivable. He should be the only person in charge of me. I should get my phone back immediately. I don't deserve any consequences after the name that barbaric woman called me.

I left out every single part of the story that implied I had done anything wrong. I left out intentionally wearing the crop top to piss her off. I left out intentionally refusing to change. I left out challenging her and implying my father would undermine her decision. I left out the hassle I was causing and threatened to make everyone late. I left out the part where I called her a bitch, which provoked her in the first place.

Liam tells me he is not going to take my phone as punishment after speaking to Grandma Judith. He says, "Two wrongs don't make a right." So what? I disrespect my stepmother, his wife, in her own house. After a not-so-quiet or secret conversation between those two, he says he is taking my phone after all. Apparently, Cara tolerates a lot, and being undermined in her house by her spouse is something she will absolutely not tolerate. "He's teaching me it's ok to be disrespectful, and there will be no consequences." Taking my phone for three days is cruel and unusual punishment. She'll pay for this.

I am the victim here. I don't have to take accountability for any of my actions because I can just spin this narrative. When people try to clear this up, to hear both sides of the story, I'll say they are victim-blaming. I'm a child, remember? I don't know right from wrong. She's supposed always to take the high road and be the bigger person. My actions shouldn't have any effect on her reactions.

This was my story, and, in my stories, I got to choose the ending. And this story ends with her being the villain.

Chapter Fifteen: Hindsight is 20/20

Fourteen Years Old: Maybe if I had worn my glasses, I would have seen this coming.

Per my usual, I am spiraling. The world doesn't stop spinning for anyone. I can barely think straight. By pushing Cara over the edge, I have broken my heart. This isn't what I wanted. This is what Amber wanted. She never loved me but would not tolerate Cara taking her place. The entire time, I thought I was the one pulling the strings. Turns out, Amber is the puppet master. I don't even want to come out of my room. I've isolated myself. I can't look Cara in the face because it hurts. Why am I like this? Why do I want to hurt other people, people who tried their best to care about me?

Cara admitted to what she did. She apologized. She cried real tears that I knew were for me. She promised she would never lash out like that again. She tried to explain that she was human. She has human emotions. Just because she's a mom, people treat her like she's not allowed to be human. She's not allowed to feel hurt and angry. She has to be at her very best at all times. Nothing less is tolerated. Why is it acceptable for everyone else to lose it, to break down, or rage, but not her? I can feel her hurt. I'm positive her heart broke a little that day as well. I believe her apology is sincere.

Over the course of the year, Cara goes out of her way to try to mend what's broken. She speaks to me, but I refuse to speak back. Amber has assured me she deserves to be punished, and I shouldn't forgive her so easily. She buys me thoughtful gifts and goodies that I never say thank you for. She continues to include me, but I refuse to join. She drives me to school, and I refuse to converse; I sit in the back seat. She cooks dinner and makes sure to make the meals I prefer. She bakes me a pumpkin cheesecake; I refuse to try even one slice. She makes special Christmas ornaments for me and hangs them on the tree; I contemplate "accidentally" knocking them onto the floor to shatter.

She even bought a book to learn how to be better. She tells me she understands now that she is an escalator and is working on learning to deal with conflicts better. If perseverance was an award, she would win it. Even though I block and avoid her, she just keeps at it, chipping away at the wall I've built.

Obeying my mother is costing me my sanity. **I feel so alone.** It eats away at me. I have to sit back and pretend I don't love her. I have to pretend she is doing this all for show, and she doesn't truly love me. I have to sit back and watch Ella and her relationship blossom while ours withers away. There are so many things I want to talk to her about. Like I finally got into a serious relationship with a guy named Daniel. He is in my grade and goes to my school. I want to tell her about my first kiss and how I feel being in love for the first time. I know better, though. If my mom caught wind that I was breaking a promise to hate Cara, I would never win her love. I have her attention, but what I really want is for her to love me. Love me the way Cara loves me.

Nothing with Amber has changed, really. She's always looking for the next easy way out. During my visit, I came to realize that she's obsessed with Cara. It's all she wants to talk about. It consumes her. I don't even hate Cara; I just love the attention I get from telling people that I hate her. I feed her what she wants to hear and some. I'm careful not to mention all the secret ways Cara makes me feel loved and wanted. I tell my mom how lonely and isolated I feel, but I do not tell her the real reason why.

Amber wants to get revenge on Liam. She says we need to hit him where it hurts. She says that she will petition the court for custody of me, and then he will have to start paying her child support again. She says all he really cares about is his money anyway. If she could start getting biweekly checks from Liam, then maybe she could finally afford to move back out of her mother's house.

Looking around my grandma's house, cluttered and constantly full of other people's kids, I don't want to give up what I have at my dad's. I don't want to live in one tiny, shared room. I don't want to give up my queen-sized bed. I don't want to give up Layla or my new relationship with Daniel. I don't want any of this.

She tells Trudy that I am going to be moving back into their house. Trudy seems excited, and that makes me feel bad. I feel bad because I don't want to live with Amber. I don't want to be here even at this moment, but I don't want to hurt Trudy's feelings. How did I get myself into this position?

Before I head home, Amber encourages me to stay on the course. She tells me to act out, don't help around their house; you don't even want to be there, let my grades drop, avoid being a part of their family. If I'm bad enough, Liam will probably just get rid of me anyway. Send me packing right back to her. She says he's lazy and won't want to fight with me…or fight for me.

Despite my negative behaviors, Liam and Cara allowed Layla to come to Tennessee with us this year. Liam says it may be better to have a friend come along. It was actually Ella who helped to badger them enough, persuading them to let her tag along. To thank Ella, I tried my best to actively leave her out of all the activities while we were there. Layla and I bunked up together. We went back to the Pigeon Forge/ Gatlinburg area, but unlike last time, they didn't have us hiking up a mountain with fictitious ice cream at the top of the five-mile hike. Zack was horsing around during that trip and almost fell off a bridge, into the river, down the mountain. Caught himself with his ankles. Lost a good hat, though.

We did a lot of shopping and eating this time around. We

went to a restaurant called "Dick's Last Resort". The staff are rude to you on purpose. When you get there, they give you a hat with an awful saying that everyone but you can see. On my hat, the waitress writes, "Plan B Poster Child." If she only knew. I bet that's what my dad is thinking now as he sits across the table from me wearing a hat that says, "I look like Deadpool without the mask."

We went on a skylift, walked on the sky bridge, and went to Ober. Ella and Layla did some ice skating up there. I just sulked on the side of the rink. I never went ice skating with them before, and now I have to pay for it by watching my best friend skating in circles with my sister, leaving me out.

The best part of the trip was seeing bears in real life. They were just walking up the mountain while we were on the skylift. While we were inside waiting to cross the bridge, filling our cups with slushies, there was a baby cub outside just wandering around. Then, on another day, while we were driving back to our cabin from town, another set of male bears was walking up the side of the mountain on the road. We caught them just as they were getting off the top of a parked Wrangler. They seemed friendly at first as they just lazily marched along the side of the road, but then they started snarling and fighting with each other. We got a video of them just putzing around.

The worst part of the trip was catching impetigo on my leg

from the sketchy hot tub. Layla's honey-crusted rash erupted first, then about a week later, mine started too. It first erupted on my left butt cheek, but then because of scratching in the night, it ended up down my leg.

The other terrible part was having a good time. Letting the fresh mountain air remind me of how wonderful it is to have the opportunity to be there. Admitting that Liam always makes sure we have the best times. He caters to me and my friends, acts goofy, makes annoyingly good dad jokes, and always has time to listen to me. And even worse, catching me, shit-eating grin, enjoying myself on camera. Proof. Proof that living with Liam and Cara has been easy and wonderful no matter what I say.

The only way I can stomach avoiding everyone at home is to pretend that I hate them all. I started to develop what Cara has termed an unhealthy codependence with Layla and Grandma Judith. Every time I get in trouble now, which seems to be most of the time nowadays, I beg Grandma Judith to just come pick me up. She's under the impression it's because I'm depressed and lonely. She thinks she is my savior. She can't understand that I'm using her. I don't really like hanging around at her house because it's in the middle of nowhere and boring. I don't have good cell reception, and she doesn't have Wi-Fi. She thinks that we are bonding. She thinks that she is healing me, and we have something special.

I don't really like being seen with her in public. I don't like the way she looks with her crazy hair. She has a smoker's cough and a wobbly knee. She wears Sketchers with extra padding on the heel. I always pray that we don't run across anyone that I know. To appease her, I suggest we go to places like the movies because the lights are out, so no one can see us together. As a bonus, I don't have to talk with her because you can't talk in a theater. I always get her to buy me gifts when we go out together, and she always obliges me because she feels pity for me and my made-up situation.

It's not truly the attention from Judith that I like the best. It's the attention that Ella is not getting that makes me happy. Judith has thrown Ella on the back burner, just like she used to do to Zack. She tells my dad and Ella that I just need extra love and attention, and so she's going to focus solely on me. She says this is fair because Ella has two parents who love her, and I don't have anybody. Anybody but Judith, that is. Liam doesn't know what to do, so he allows this. He even starts letting her schedule a visit with me every Wednesday. And just like the post office, she shows up rain or shine. She even attempted to drive through a blizzard to get me. The more Cara and Liam argue about how Judith is treating Ella, leaving her out, the more I want to ask Judith to get me. It makes Ella feel like the second best for once. She should know what it feels like to be unwanted.

Judith won't let it go. She's become obsessed with Cara as well. She brings up her calling me a cunt every time that we are together. It's been almost a year, but she refuses to let it go and convinces me that I haven't moved past it either. She leads me, like a lawyer would a witness, into agreeing that she probably calls me other names, downgrades me, and knit-picks everything I do. Judith makes me feel the way Amber does. I feel like I have to continue to talk poorly about Cara if I intend to keep her love and attention.

I tell her what I know she wants to hear. I tell her that Cara and Ella always gossip about me. Things are worse than ever and each day I live there is a struggle. It's like I'm losing my will to live. I'm just so depressed. I stay in my room all the time. I say these things so many times that I start to believe them. Convincing her is brainwashing me. I've lost touch with reality. I don't even know what is real now and what I have made up; it's all blurred.

Blurred. Believe me when I say everything around me is blurred. Quite literally. They did a vision screen at school, and I can't see anything. Cara took me to get an official eye exam with the optometrist, and he gave me the worst news of my teenage life. I need to wear glasses. I can't be seen in glasses. I will look like a real loser. I went from a DUFF to a four-eyed freak just like that. I tried on so many glasses from the wall of frames. I tried to find some of the most expensive frames they sold. If I have to wear glasses, they might as well be the best. Of course, I don't plan to wear the glasses. I plan to waste Cara and Liam's money and then conveniently "forget" to wear them as Lauren does.

On the way home from my appointment, I asked Cara how long I was supposed to wear the glasses. She seems confused. She asked me what I meant. She says, "Like for the rest of your life." WHAT!? I can't be seen in glasses for the rest of my life. Glasses are for nerds, not baddies. Why is this happening to me? I tell her I thought that you just "wore glasses for a little while, and they fixed your eyes." She laughed out loud. She told me these are glasses, not braces. She asked why I would think that. She said, "If they fixed your vision, why do you think that old people wear glasses"? I mean, I guess she has worn glasses the entire time I have known her. I just thought she liked them and made her look smarter.

I wasn't prepared for this. On top of that, I was feeling dumb. I asked her if I just wear them all the time. I asked, "Do I wear them in the shower"? She responded that "normal people don't, but you can if you want". She was making fun of me. Sometimes, I liked to pretend that I was dumber than I was, but I didn't like to feel dumb, especially in front of Cara. It made me feel vulnerable. That is an emotion I don't like to acknowledge.

I tried to avoid wearing my glasses every chance I got. I even tried convincing Liam that I didn't really need them. I told him that I could see just fine without them and that I would start wearing them when things worsened. Maybe I would have seen this next part coming if I had just started wearing my glasses. Maybe with my glasses, I could have seen the red flags.

Amber and Judith are draining my life. It's a relief when I can get away from them. I don't know what I'd do if I didn't have Layla. I feel like I'm a live wire, and she's there to ground me. She never wants to talk about Cara unless I bring her up. Layla is self-absorbed and usually just talks about herself. Even that I can deal with, with her, I can talk about the things I want to talk about, like Daniel.

He's not exactly what I thought having a boyfriend would be like. At school, he treats me like crap in front of his friends. Tells everyone I am just dating him because I want to be a "Hot Cheeto Girl". I'll save you a Google search; it's not a compliment. He insults me right to my face, and I am expected to just laugh it off. A Hot Cheeto Girl is someone who acts loud, is bitchy, and rude for no reason. They try to act "ghetto," always up in someone else's business, don't do their homework, and pretend to be obsessed with hot chips/Cheetos. He's not wrong. That is a description of the new me.

He's broken things off with me several times. Shamefully, I begged him to take me back. He does for a while. When it's good, it's good. I want to believe we are in love. I don't want to lose him. We talk all night; I just stay on the phone and listen to him play the game in the background, if I'm honest. He doesn't sit with me at lunch because he says I dress embarrassingly, and he can't let his boys see him with someone like that. I wish Cara would understand why I need those shirts.

I have to listen to specific music to be with him. I have to like certain foods. He makes fun of me when I haven't seen certain movies, so I spend my weekends in my room freshening up on the movies he enjoys and quotes. He thinks wearing Converse high tops is for losers. His girl is only supposed to wear Nike Blazers and Jordan's. It's hard for me to live up to his expectations.

Layla's dad bought her the Jordan's for her back-to-school shoes. My birthday is coming up, but Liam informed me that I will not be getting those shoes. I am desperate to have them. He just doesn't understand. Cara says they are over budget. That's why he won't buy them! My birthday budget is $100. The shoes are running around $400-$500. If Mr. Highland can buy Layla these shoes, I don't understand why they can't buy them for me. My dad says I can buy them myself if I get enough birthday money or save up.

Layla told me about a site where I can get the Jordan's cheap. She bought her shoes at the mall but says this site is legit. They were only $150. My budget is $100; I know if I tell Judith, she will sneak extra birthday money to make sure that I can buy them. It ended up taking 10-12 weeks to get my shoes. They shipped from China. They were fake. Dad said, "Sorry, kiddo". They look real, and no one is going to be able to tell the difference. Cara said I should have known they would be fake from a site selling them for $300 less than retailed. I double-checked sites that show you how to tell a fake shoe. Just my luck, they ARE fake. Daniel says he is a sneaker head. If I go to school in fake Jordan's, he'll probably dump me immediately. What a waste.

Worse than fake shoes, I keep getting this terrible feeling that Daniel is cheating on me. I have been tracking him on his phone, and it turns out he is not always where he says he is. He also keeps turning off his location. I knew I wasn't enough for him. I knew that he would leave me. No one ever chooses me. I am leftovers. I have my friends searching around the school for him, stalking him like I do. He gets annoyed when he catches them taking his picture in the hallway. He told me to tell them to stop, or he **was** going to break up with me again.

Layla tells me that she heard that he is cheating on me. She knows the girl that he is talking to behind my back. Probably meeting up with her. I searched for the girl on social media. Before long, I found myself stalking her, too. I am way better looking than she is. She must be giving him something that I'm not. If it weren't for Liam and all his rules, I could be alone with him. Then maybe he would choose me after all.

Grandma Judith says real love is worth fighting for. I get the impression she means physically fighting for. I'm not doing that again. Lesson learned. I want to ask Cara what she would do, but I don't want to admit I need her. I consciously have decided not to ask my mom for motherly advice, especially about boys. She has never been good at keeping one. Besides, I don't want her to know that Daniel is cheating on me or that maybe he never loved me at all. I want to keep up this persona that every guy at the school thinks I am hot. That is what I have been telling her, knowing I would never have to prove it.

I accuse Daniel of cheating on me over the phone. He denies it. *I'm delusional.* For once, he is upset. He says something is wrong with me; I make things up in my head and then believe it. Fed up, I told him I would break up with him this time. It sounds like he is crying. Maybe he does love me. Before we hang up, I tell him I've changed my mind, and I want to stay with him. He must promise not to talk with Marissa anymore. I can't lose Daniel. He's the only guy showing me any interest right now. If I'm not his girlfriend, then I am nothing. I have no other interests or hobbies. I don't play any sports. I am just Daniel's girlfriend. If we break up, I am just another face in the hall, a nobody.

Karma is serving me the chaos I deserve. Layla decided to try out and has been playing on the basketball team while I was planning Cara's undoing. She has been hanging out with another girl, Kendall. She has been staying with Layla while I have been entertaining my mother. Layla has been less supportive of me. I thought she told me I should live with my mom because she believed all my lies. I thought she was genuinely concerned for me. Now I know it's because she was over me. She was replacing me. Kendall is all she talks about now. Kendall is always at her house when I get there. Kendall, Kendall, Kendall. It makes me sick. All the things we have been through together, and she just tosses me aside. I just feel like I can't take another loss.

The Winter Carnival is coming up. I want to go to the dance with Daniel. I want him to wrap his arms around my body and slide his hands over my skin. Touch me anywhere he wants. I want to prove to him that I can be the girl he wants. I want to buy a dress that is skintight and dips into a deep V to show off some cleavage. I know Cara will not purchase a dress like that for me. Layla and Lillian showed me dresses that they have and helped me pick one out. My dad says I can go to the carnival and the dance. He pre-paid for the tickets for both Daniel and me. Layla and her date are going to dinner before the dance. It will be a double date. I'll bring Daniel along. Perfect plan, except when I ask for another $50, Liam tells me he's not giving me that much for dinner. He is such a dick. I'll have to ask Judith.

On the day of the dance, I put on my dress, it's tight, just the way I wanted. When I look in the mirror, my stomach bloats out. I can see my belly button indent through the dress. I look disgusting. I have to look like this because Cara couldn't just mind her business and let me starve myself. I'm not going. Lillian can have her dress back. There is no way I will be seen in public like this. One look at me in this dress, and Daniel will notice how good every other girl looks in her dress. I tell my dad I'm not going to the dance and I will just go to my Grandma Amanda's house. It was my mom's weekend anyway.

Now that you've heard the truth, it is just a smidge different than the version I have prepared for everyone else. In Judith's version, Liam refused to pay for anything. I couldn't go because he couldn't be bothered to give me any money. In the L version, my dad and I got into a nasty fight. He grounded me and forbade me from going to the dance as punishment. He was forcing me to go to my mom's for the weekend.

I had to call my mom. She was not expecting me this weekend. It's not like she had a job, but I felt like I was inconveniencing her by deciding to come at the last minute. I could tell she was irritated, so I gave her what she wanted. Crocodile tears. I wanted to go to the dance so bad. He told me I could go at first, but today, he changed his mind at the last minute, and now I can't go. Layla's mom bought me a dress because he wouldn't. I wasted her money, and the dress is nonrefundable. He is ruining my life.

I was expecting her to pity me and just agree to meet him at the carpool lot like always. I was not expecting her to call him. Amber had perfected talking about Liam, but she never spoke to him and tried to work something out like a co-parent. Imagine the surprise when he heard the version of the story that she was repeating to him. He set her straight and then turned around and set me straight for lying to her in the first place. He told her not only that he had told me I could go, but that he had already purchased the tickets and that I was wasting that money. He told her I was lying about the dress; it wasn't purchased just for me; I was just borrowing it from Lillian, and I could just return it to her. Catching me in this lie changed the trajectory I had Liam set for. I had unintentionally planted the first seed of suspicion.

By the time I got back from her house at the end of the weekend, I had more explaining to do. Lillian had asked Ella what happened at our house and why my dad wouldn't let me go to the dance. Ella told her that nothing happened. She told her I was lying, like usual, and made the whole story up. Lillian was flabbergasted. She couldn't believe I had made up such an elaborate story. She couldn't understand why I didn't just say I didn't want to go. She started wondering what else I made up. She started thinking back to every interaction she had had with Cara. Something was off. Cara was always so nice and inviting. She had never witnessed problems between us or heard Cara make sideway comments.

My dad spoke to Judith about the incident. He couldn't believe I had gone to such great lengths to make everyone think he was a bad guy. He told Judith I was lying. He told her the same thing that he told my mother. Judith came to my defense and brought up the dinner money. He told Judith she was acting crazy now. He said it didn't matter where we went for dinner; chicken tenders didn't cost $50 at a single restaurant in this city. He never said I couldn't go to dinner. He simply wouldn't give me twice the money I needed to eat. Arguing with Judith didn't confuse him the way it normally did for my benefit. It unintentionally started opening his eyes to what was going on. For the first time, he was seeing the tip of the iceberg of the manipulation I had been controlling Judith with for the last year.

Monday morning, first thing, Daniel found me at my locker and said we needed to talk. I thought he was upset that I had ditched him at the last minute at the dance. That wasn't it at all. He told me that after this semester ended, he would not be returning to the school. He said that he was switching high schools. I could feel the panic setting in. He reassured me that our love was strong enough to survive a long-distance relationship. I wanted to believe him.

In the months to come, Daniel started becoming more distant from me. I could feel him pushing me away. He still indulged me with attention at night. He whispered sweet nothings into my ear through the phone before I had to hang up. He hadn't sent me a candy gram candy cane the week before break. I sent one to him but didn't receive one in return. I don't understand what was going wrong. We loved each other. I had Layla and Kendall prowl around the school at lunch, looking for him. I hoped he wasn't exchanging a gift or candy gram with Marissa. He was with his friend Dylan. Layla snapped a picture of them and sent it to me. Her flash was on. He was pissed. He sent me a text stating enough was enough with my crazy mind games and obsession. He was done with me.

After school, I raced out to the line of buses. I spotted him before he made it to his bus. When I grabbed his shoulder, and he turned around, seeing me, he pushed me away. The crowd was staring at us. He told me I was certifiable. He was done with me. I was trash. He called me an ugly bitch in front of the entire school. Told me to lose his number. I was frantic. There was no way this was happening. Later, after exactly 14 calls, he answered his phone. Exasperation in his voice. I feigned innocence. Layla had gone rogue and took his picture without me knowing. I prostrated before his figurative feet and begged for one last chance.

He granted me another chance, but it wasn't even a full week into the second semester before Daniel started acting differently towards me. He left my text messages on read for hours. He wasn't readily available for my phone calls. He didn't want to stay up all night talking to me on the phone. By the following week, he stopped talking to me altogether. He had blocked me on all his social media accounts. I was devastated and desperate. I had friends of friends checking his Instagram for me. I had Ella stalking his pages. He had found a new girlfriend in just two weeks. She didn't look anything like me. Deranged, I asked Ella if his new girlfriend was an upgrade from me. Begging her with my eyes to say no. She obliged. I needed to get him back. I knew where he worked. Every night, I tried convincing my dad to take me out to get a donut to cheer me up. If he could just see me again, in person, he would change his mind. I stalked his new girlfriend. I tried to spread rumors to get them to break up. Nothing was working.

I was numb.

I skipped class to see the counselor. She was short with a witch nose and short, choppy hair. She wore plain polo shirts and cargo pants. Ewe. I cried my eyes out in her office, snorting all over the sleeves of my zip-up before she offered me a tissue. She wasn't a very warm person for a counselor. She told me that high school love is puppy love. It never matures into anything sustainable, but it was okay to grieve the loss of a loved one. She was supposed to advise me on how to win him back, not telling me to arrange our love funeral.

Couples lined the halls, holding hands, sneaking pecks on the lips, laughing into each other's arms. No one even glanced my way. I was invisible. Now that I wasn't Daniel's girl, I might as well disappear. I felt empty but full of sadness at the same time. This is why there are so many country songs about heartbreaks.

When old people are in love, and one dies, the other dies too shortly after. They die from a broken heart. Wanting to die in peace, I lay in my bed, face down on the mattress, the bars of my headboard imprinting into my forehead. I lifted my face to reposition my neck, and through the crack of the mattress, I saw a folded-up piece of paper under my bed. Like a lunatic, I thought, "it's a letter from Daniel". I could have tousled my entire bed just to get to that wad of paper. When I unfolded it, this is what I read:

Ava,

If you are reading this note, please know that you are loved. You are beautiful. You are smart. You are enough. You have me. Please, let your guard down. Let me love you. Let me be the mother I know I am. You are my daughter; I have raised and loved you through all the good and challenging times. You deserve to feel special. You deserve to feel like you belong. I don't want you to be alone. You have me. If you need someone to lean on, to bear the weight, I'm here. I'll wait as long as it takes for you to come around because you are worth it. I could just tell you I love you, but that's not enough. I wanted to write it down. That way, if you feel down and lonely, you can just look back at these words and know that you don't have to do things alone. It doesn't matter what opinion anyone has about you. They do not define you.

Leftovers

You are loved.

You are beautiful.

You are smart.

You are strong.

You are Enough.

With love now and for Always,

Cara

Chapter Sixteen: Breaking the Broken

Pity and Friendship are Two Passions that are Incompatible with Each Other

I'm whining. How could she possibly have known this is what I needed to hear today, of all days? How could she stand to love me after what I had done to her? She loves me without stipulations. I've gone too far. I don't know how to right the wrong I've caused. I can't love her out loud. Where this note should have helped heal me, it's left me even more heartbroken, knowing she is offering a love I can't accept.

Layla says I am such a downer. She decides I need to be refreshed. She will be at high school next year and says we need to get ready for the wild times before us. She says this summer will be a "hot girl summer". You would think this means we will tan, get in shape, follow some beauty routines. You would be mistaken. She wants to play a game this summer. Because we are hot girls, we are going to compete to do *hot* stuff with guys. We drag out a notebook and start jotting down various favors; if you will, we can do to earn points. The highest score will be declared the hottest girl of the summer.

Holding hands in public – 1pt

Kissing on the lips- 3pts

Letting him grab your boobs- 3pts

French kissing- 5pts

Secret hickey- 5pts

Getting fingered- 10 pts

Hand job- 10pts

Blow job- 20pts – additional 5pts if you swallow.

Losing your virginity- 50 pts

You had to keep track of the person, in case it needed to be verified, and your points. You couldn't keep getting points if it was the same person. For instance, if I kissed Daniel twice, I still only got 3 pts. I would have to kiss Daniel and a different boy if I wanted 6pts. This was going to be a challenge, alright. I can't get Liam to leave me alone with a boy for over 3 minutes. He isn't going to let me go to their house. Now that I am grudgingly single, I won't feel guilty about adding on points, but it would have been easier to get the highest-valued points if I was still with him.

Unlike the vape, I don't want Ella to know anything about this challenge. There is no way she would agree to play. She would run straight to Cara and Dad. I phase her out of the L's lives…and mine. Since we will all be in high school, except Ella, I tell her that Laura, Lillian, and Layla all sat me down and told me not to invite Ella over anymore. She was too young and immature, and they didn't want to hang out with her. She was too much of a nuisance. Ella was hurt and didn't understand why they would say that because, other than Layla occasionally, they had always been so nice to her. Whenever one of the L's asked about Ella, I told them she was too busy to hang out, she wasn't home, or she had other friends over. This was a temporary fix, but all I could manage with all my other scheming at the time.

Cara has asked me to make dinner with her, and I'm going to do it for the first time in a long time. No one has to know that I am playing both sides. I will continue to tell Amber and Judith how terrible my life is, but at the same time, I will enjoy the time and attention Cara dedicates to me. She doesn't make a big deal, which is good since I'm trying to be low-key about enjoying her company. As a plus, she doesn't let Ella help; it's just for the two of us. It's a win-win for me.

Over the summer, I go between Liam's and my Grandma Amanda's houses. My mom told me she had filed a petition with the court to get me back. Hearing her say these official words out loud is relieving. This is what I have been wanting. Not to live with her, but for her to WANT me to live with her. It feels more real now. She says that because I am 14, the court will ask me who I want to live with. It will be easy to get custody because all I have to do is tell the judge I want to live with her, and voila, the court will give her custody.

Until then, she asked if I had any birthday money left or from Judith. She says she needs it because she needs gas money. She doesn't wait for me to answer; she just gets into my purse, pulls out the $34 I have left, and takes it for herself. It won't always be this way, her taking everything from me. Once she gets custody, she will be in a better position to care for me. Then, she can start paying me back. She can start saving up to buy me things for my birthday and Christmas that didn't come from the sale section of Dollar General.

Within the one week I am gone, Layla has already scored 14 pts. I'm still at zero. She met up at the rink with some guys from school with Kendall. I want to tell her that I think I may be going to live with my mom after all. As I am about to confide this in her, I see the necklace swinging across her collarbone. BFF bedazzled. I look over at Kendall, and she has the twin sitting across her neck. I don't want to tell her anything else to make her closer to Kendall. I tell her I feel nauseated and leave. I do feel sick, sick of her always choosing someone else over me.

Summer flies by. My attitude worsens. Now that I know I will be moving in with my mom, I don't have any reason to act right.

There will be no consequences where I am going. I throw a temper tantrum whenever I am asked to leave my room. It will be easier to leave if I start detaching myself now. Between Daniel leaving me in pieces and Layla putting a deep freeze on our relationship so she can be with Kendall, I am starting to think I am depressed. For real now, it's not just what I tell Judith to make her feel needed.

Maybe earning some points will make me feel better. Daniel lives across the street from Dakota. I haven't talked to her in a long time. I called her up and asked if I could come hang out. Layla is with Kendall anyway. Dakota seems shocked to hear from me but is eager to have me come over. I put on a short sundress and put on my Converse shoes. It feels good to be able to wear them again. Part of me wants to change them, because I'm hoping to see Daniel, not Dakota. I don't have any other shoes to wear with the sundress, though. It will look crappy with my black Nike slides or dirty white Crocs. I brush my hair out of my sloppy trash bun. I feel pretty. Hopefully, it's pretty enough to entice Daniel to help me win a game.

Cara drives me to Dakota's. I am nervous and paranoid. I worry that she knows what I am up to. She gave me a suspicious look when she saw how dressed up I was to go to Dakota's. I've never dressed up to hang out with her before. I'm not even there 5 minutes before I begin badgering Dakota about Daniel. Is he home? Does he ever have anyone over? She seemed confused because I was so obsessed with him. I forget that I've been playing shadow with

Layla and haven't spent real time talking or hanging out with Dakota. She has no idea that he is my ex.

The bomb drops. She tells me that he asked her out a little while back. She hung out with him once but didn't like him. I feel instantly defensive. How could she think that the love of my life wasn't good enough for her? It would have been a privilege for a girl like her to be asked out by a guy like him. Despite my best efforts to hide these emotions, I feel like she knows. Hurriedly, she remarks that he's not home and then quickly changes the subject.

Cara couldn't come back to get me fast enough. It was like hearing a firework go off a few feet away from you. My hearing was muffled, and it felt like I was underwater. I could see Dakota talking, but I wasn't comprehending anything she was saying. Circling back to him, asking her out was the only thing I could accomplish. Why her? Why was scrawny Dakota a viable option, but returning to me was not? Why wasn't I good enough? I crawled into bed and imagined I was shrinking down and folding up to fit back into my Tupperware bowl. Eventually, everyone forgets about me and finds something or someone new.

***

When a sequoia tree finally falls, you may hear some crackling as the wood splits, but for the most part, no one knows or takes a second to mourn its death. Something so grand, finally having the life sucked out of it from disease and trauma, and no one cares. That is how it feels when my heart's very last muscular fibers tear. I'll spare you the insane and dramatic details that lead up to this tragedy.

Layla had turned on me. She gave up on me. She had skillfully disintegrated the glue that bound us together. She believes there is something wrong with me. I was some weirdo she had taken under her wing, and now I am jealous and possessive, and she's had enough of my self-pity. She accuses me of being obsessed with her. She alleges that I don't want to be her friend; I want to be her girlfriend. She says that she doesn't belong to me. She doesn't need my permission to hang around other people. She's sick of my controlling and jealous behavior.

The fight erupted after I found out she had unofficially given Kendall a room in their house since she was always there. Layla's brother had moved out, so Layla thought it would be amazing if she decorated the room and Kendall could have that space for herself. "She was more like a sister than just a friend." Layla thought she should move in because they were such great friends. They were in sync. She never offered me a room in her house. I couldn't even have one drawer in her dresser for the things I brought over.

To set the record straight, Layla did not break up with me. I broke up with her. I couldn't take sharing her anymore. I felt like we were a married couple, and she was the partner who couldn't keep their hands to themselves. She just kept "cheating" on me over and over. She never loved me. This was an unbreakable pattern. No matter how good I was to her, how much I conformed to her requests, I would never be good enough for her. I was never going to be enough. She had an insatiable appetite for attention. I couldn't blackmail my way back into her heart this time.

This time, when I cried to Lillian, she wouldn't hear it. I tried explaining that Layla had changed and was a terrible version of herself. I was the victim. She had given up on me when I needed her the most. She was the worst kind of friend. She was a self-centered ball of destruction. She was a lying bitch and a slut.

Lillian came off her chair so fast that it startled me. She told me to get out of her house. She was always so levelheaded and calm that I wasn't sure if this was something I was hallucinating or if it was real. It was so unexpected.

"No one was going to talk about her sister like that." She didn't care what Layla had supposedly done. She was done with me, too. She wanted me out of her house and out of their lives. She was sick of my "oh woe is me" attitude and lies. She called me a hypocrite. She accused me of doing what Layla did to me, to

everyone around me. She asked me how Trudy feels when I never speak to her unless I am upset with Ella. She asked me how I thought Dakota felt when I left her to chase after her sister in the first place. Hell, I only ever came around her when Layla was too busy for me. And that was why I was here now, wasn't it? If I wanted a pity party, I was going to have to reserve a table for one because she was fed up.

HOW DARE SHE!? Who the fuck did they think they were? You can't talk to me like that. I wanted to burn everything she had ever given me, trash, and cut holes in everything I had borrowed. I wanted to scream out loud. I wanted to punch something. I felt rage and turmoil. I hated her. I hated them. I wanted to shake her by her shoulders so she could feel my unsettling feelings. Nothing felt like this, a woman scorned. I wanted to obliterate her.

No, I didn't. I wanted to curl up and die. I was in physical pain; my body ached and shivered. I felt weak, deserted, and fragile. I just wanted everything to stop. My eyes stung, and I felt like I was still crying without any tears left to fall. My legs gave out minutes ago. I was face down in my bed. I couldn't stand the smell of her hair on my pillowcase. At the same time, I hoped the smell would never fade away. I wanted to be reminded that we were real; we had something real. By breaking up with Layla, I had done an unimaginable thing. I had broken myself, severed the last thread that held me together. I had broken the broken.

Chapter Seventeen: Teeter Totter

15 years old

I can't take it anymore. I have been doing everything she's asked, and I get nothing in return except broken promises. I should have known better. She hasn't kept a single promise to me my entire life. It's been months, and still no word. I could feel that there was no upcoming court date in my disintegrating heart. The new me was Ballsey. So, I just asked her straight up. It turns out that she never even filled out the paperwork, let alone filed it. She lied straight to my face. They told me not to get my panties in a bunch; it wasn't even that big of a deal. Besides, the paperwork "had to be perfect," which would take some time.

I know why she hasn't been keeping her promises to me. She found another guy online to date, Steve. At first glance, Steve is a normal person. He hasn't been in jail yet. That's a new characteristic for one of her boyfriends. He's not violent, and he doesn't do drugs. He doesn't have any baggage himself, no crazy baby mamas or kids that he left and moved on from. That's kind of the scary part. If he was "normal," what would be the appeal of dating Amber? She has nothing to offer in a relationship. She has three children, all fathered by different men. She doesn't have a job, nor does she want one. She doesn't have her place to stay or a car. She "let herself go" and was at least 100 pounds overweight now. She doesn't volunteer her time. She doesn't have any secret awesome talents. Frankly, it makes no sense that he would want to be in a relationship with her.

Steve is apparently on social security disability. I swear she must have access to a database that can filter down options to felons, psychiatric patients, and men who qualify for a steady SSI/SSD check. I can see why she would want to date him. I don't like the way he looks at Trudy. It makes me feel like she is not safe. Sometimes, I can feel his eyes bouncing off my flesh. I hope that her having children, whom she doesn't supervise, isn't the reason he was interested in her. I hear sometimes pedophiles do that. They find a vulnerable woman with kids and date her to get closer to the children. They are playing chess, while she thinks they are playing checkers.

If she was going to break a promise to me, then I was breaking my deal with her. Over the next several months, I started interacting with Cara every chance that I got. Of course, I was still doing this secretly, behind Liam's back. When he was mandated and kept over at work, I would come downstairs and hang out. I would linger and engage with Cara, laugh, and chat about things at school. It reminded me of when I was nine years old, sitting on the end of her bed. She was so easy to talk to. I missed this. I missed having a mom who would listen to me without expectations for what I would say or the consequences for saying things she didn't want to hear.

Not only did I join her in going out to the store, to movies, and dinner, but I also sat up front in the passenger's seat, right next to her (in Ella's spot). I even thought about reaching over and placing my hand on her. Holding hands wasn't just for couples. I could hold my mom's hand if I wanted to. It was like I was living a secret double life like you see in the movies. It felt like I was getting away with something, even though everything we did was normal for a mother and daughter. I don't always wait for an invitation either; sometimes I would suggest that we go and do things like get our nails done or go see the movie, and she would just take us. Why couldn't I appreciate her for what she was: a good mom?

She did all the grunt work. She worked full-time as a nurse practitioner, but she also did everything around the house for us. She planned the dinner, cooked, did all the shopping, helped do all the homework, planned all the trips, cleaned the house, attended to the animals, and still made time to do extracurricular activities with us. She made all the appointments and organized everything in our lives. She gave everything she had to this family. We are her priority. I am a priority to her, not like Amber.

Maybe that's why Amber despises her. My mother has no motherly instincts. She is not motivated in life to want better or to be better. She truly isn't doing herself any favors by comparing herself to Cara. Low-key, it makes me feel embarrassed for her, just thinking about how she "stacks up" against Cara.

I'm coasting through. Amber wants me to start using the counselor at school as a ruse. She wants me to start feeding the counselor lies about how Cara and Liam treat me. I go to the counselor's office often, like every last block, biology class, but rather than talking about Cara and Liam, I mostly just cry about Daniel. She feeds me peppermints, and I tell her I am empty inside. Without Layla, Lillian, or Daniel, I don't have any self-worth. I don't even know who I am. Every so often, the counselor nods that she is listening and tells me that what I am experiencing is normal. Is ruining my own life with poor decisions and creating collateral damage for everyone around me normal? I'm pretty sure she doesn't listen to anything I say, but it gets me out of Biology and Amber off my back.

I want to be done with Amber. If you are a nerd, you may appreciate this. She reminds me of a queen spider from the Forgotten Realms, Lolth. Lolth is this cruel leader. The Dungeon and Dragons geeks say she thrives in a dark abyss. She revels in "betrayal and bloodshed". Amber and Lolth have many similarities. They both demand fidelity and admiration despite their wickedness. You must never question their motives or challenge their decisions. If you follow them blindly, you will be in absolute carnage. I'm on her web. I can feel the spindles of thread that connect us. I'm bonded and shackled to her. The more I try to wriggle away, the tighter she winds the threads to try to pull me back, closer.

One evening, dad dragged me across town after school for an appointment. Cara and he found me a new counselor, not through the school. Cara and he had already met with him. I was going to meet with him today. From what I gathered, Judith was convinced I was depressed and barely holding onto the will to live. My mother told Liam to have me tested for drug use. Cara suspects I am harboring deep-rooted abandonment issues from my mother. She has convinced Dad that I have developed unhealthy behaviors and poor coping strategies. I overheard her telling him she was worried I was developing a disorder, histrionic personality disorder, to be exact. He agrees with her. He thinks there is something wrong with me.

And now, here it is; I've snapped right back to where I was. I'm on a teeter-totter of mind fuckery. In one moment, I know and understand that my dad and Cara are doing their best. They are loving and helping to guide me to being a functional member of society. Then, I slam back down to the ground. Everything is their fault. Amber just understands me better and lets me be my true self. There is nothing wrong with me; it's them. I don't have abandonment issues. I'm not crazy. My childhood has nothing to do with me now. It's impossible to believe both are true at once. I have lost control.

Everything is wreckage around me. My teenage life is a wasteland. There is utter destruction. No one trusts anyone, and the backstabbing is almost literal rather than figurative. Every person I have had a relationship with has been contaminated by my curse. It's hard to breathe when I am around or even when my name is spewed from someone's lips. The air is simply that thick. Intentionally corrupting stories about anyone who's crossed me is now a specialty. I am a chef serving the crowd.

Layla has betrayed me. I let everyone know that she indeed won our little competition. A whore. Embarrassed to find that Liam found my notebook detailing our point system. Embarrassed that Cara knows. Even worse, she made me admit to it in front of Judith.

I had told Judith that Layla was a slut after we broke off our friendship. I didn't elaborate, and Judith didn't ask. Now after Judith has been coming over, trying to have a family intervention where she thinks she's some sort of mediator, she hears there is no truth in my stories. She insisted that Liam should let me have more freedom and go more places, and then Cara said that I couldn't be trusted and told me to tell Judith why. "Tell her about the challenges you have with your friends. About all the nasty things you want to try to do with boys for points". Staring straight into her face, I lied. I proclaimed that I wasn't embarrassed. I was even proud.

The look on Judith's face when she asked me if I really did suck a boy's dick for points destroyed any confidence I held during the argument. She tried her best to hold a poker face while she awaited my answer. She tried her best not to show the absolute disappointment she had for me at that moment. I felt sleazy. I felt like I deserved a look of disgrace. But as you imagined, I would never admit that.

I backpedaled, telling everyone that it was all Layla. It was her idea, and as they say, misery likes company. I guess so do sluts. She didn't want to go down alone for something this atrocious. I agreed to play but didn't do anything on the list (not for a lack of trying). She was a whore, and I basically watched her lose her virginity in front of me for 50 points. That was an outright lie, but I needed to deflect the disgust and horror in the room from me and displace it onto someone else.

Lillian won't acknowledge or appease me. Daniel is never coming back. Ella doesn't need me anymore; she can't even stand to be around me. She has grown into a "normal" healthy teenager. She doesn't try to fit into conforms and is happy being herself. She doesn't have to dress, talk, and act like her friends to be their friends. When someone doesn't respond to her messages or say they are taking a break from their friendship, she lets them go. She doesn't beg them to come back. It's like she understands no one can define her, and their opinions of her don't dictate her opinion of herself. It sickens me. I want her to feel the disgrace I feel.

Liam has chosen Cara over me. He won't leave her. He

won't even consider it. Their marriage isn't on the rocks. It's stronger than it was 3 years before now. They are both making conscious efforts to be a better partner to one another. Better communication has dismantled the illusions I created for Liam. He understands what I have been doing to deceive everyone about Cara. He can see that I am shifting the target to him now. He thinks I'm damaged goods. Cara thinks I need a damn psychiatrist. After speaking with Liam and Cara, Grandma Judith is confused. She wants some answers to why I have been lying. I have no one on my side. The counselor suggested at the very first session that I may be the problem in my own life.

After finding out that Cara shared the secret about our little rendezvous, everyone wanted answers. Liam wanted to know, if I truly felt uncomfortable and unloved by Cara, targeted even, then why was I spending so much time with her when he was away? Judith wanted the same answers. Apparently, Cara had been writing all the effort she was putting in in a journal. Judith wanted to know why I never told her about any of these positive changes. She didn't know anything about the love letters, the hanging out, the hugs, the "I love you" texts exchanged. She couldn't understand why I had been hiding the truth. Amber was literally the only one left that I didn't feel humiliated by. Everyone could see me for who I was, a liar. Amber was the only one who didn't care. She actually preferred me this way.

Amber told me not to go back to the counselor. Make something up. Tell Liam I didn't like seeing a man, and I only wanted a female therapist. She said this one was already tainted by knowing my back story (the chaotic childhood she gifted me). If I kept my word this time, she would work on filling out the paperwork after all. It will look better to the judge if I am not in counseling anyway. She will tell the judge that I have been emotionally and verbally abused over the course of the last eight years, and Liam has failed to put me in counseling despite her frequent requests. It's a lie. In court, though, it will be her word against his. I muddled over my options, and just like that, I was trapped like a fly in her web, ready to be devoured. I did exactly that. It was unfathomable the power she held over me. She made my decisions for me, and I followed through with them whether I truly wanted to or not.

Liam was no longer lenient. He expected respect and obedience as well. He started enforcing the rules, checking in on my chores, and following through with punishments when I gave him attitude. The last ship of pity had sailed, and he didn't even bother buying a ticket anymore. Liam told Judith that she was not a therapist, and over the last year, she had only made the situation worse. My attitude was nothing but worse, and she needed to stay in her lane. She was not a parent in his household. Being told she couldn't take me alone anymore infuriated Judith. She was his mother, after all. She made the rules for him, not this way around.

That bought me Judith's loyalty again. She was ready to follow me back down the rabbit hole. She was devastated by my dad separating us.

Despite my behaviors, I was regressing due to Amber's invisible chokehold on me. Cara and Dad were still offering me opportunities to make my life more enjoyable and easier. I was 15 years old now, and despite borderline failing grades in a few classes, Dad told me he would enroll me in driver's training. He specifically informed me that Cara was against the idea and felt that it was a privilege that should be earned. As of right now, constantly bickering, hiding in my room, occasionally telling him I hated him, and starting to fail classes, I absolutely was not earning this privilege. He was more optimistic. He thought if he gave me things, I would act better. He was wrong. Cara chastised him for this.

Even after her disagreement, she agreed that I would be turning 16 in just six months, and they bought me a car. They said I needed to get my act together, and then, poof, it would be mine on my birthday. It was nice; an all-wheel drive SUV with leather seats, a backup camera, and third-row seating. Dad got a good deal from a friend, but he did leave some trash in it. I was so excited. I never wanted to clean anything up more in my whole life. I happily picked the littered trash out from in between and beneath the seats of what was going to be my new ride. I had a car, keys just waiting to be handed over, and I hadn't even started driver's training yet.

My mom says I shouldn't have accepted the driver's training offer or the car from Liam. She says taking gifts from him makes me weak. He can hold it over my head later and pretend that he is a good dad when he's not. If I would have just waited until "tax time" she could have tried to get me a car. If I had a car, I could get a job. She jokes that I could start helping her pay the child support she owes Liam once I started getting a steady paycheck. She laughed after the comment, but I'm not sure if she was really joking or if she was throwing a line out to see if I would bite.

I think she is getting worried about money. She is pregnant yet again. Steve has been causing problems between them. She says that he keeps trying to discipline Trudy and Issac (my little brother) and she's not having it. He thinks that he is better than her. Tells her she's not being a good parent and she needs to be more active in her children's lives. He's sick of them cussing and carrying on without any consequences. She tells me that Steve is the problem. It's really that she can't take any accountability for her poor parenting.

Steve tries to talk to me in private sometimes. He tells me that I am lucky I am living with Liam. Steve told me that he's not about to let Amber raise his kid. He's thinking about leaving her when the baby is born, taking his kid, and running. I want to tell Amber that Steve is conspiring against her, but deep down, I know it would be right for him to do. Besides, she would probably just call me a liar anyway. Tell me that I am just trying to ruin this for her.

She's made that opinion very clear in the past.

Since things were still spiraling, and I was throwing more temper tantrums than ever before, my dad tried yet again to get me into another counselor. He had been calling around, but apparently, there were long waitlists for adolescent therapists. It was almost comforting to know that I wasn't the only person struggling with interpersonal turmoil. It was actually Cara who called around to find another counseling service. She found a therapist who could get me in almost right away, but they were requesting written consent signed by both Liam and Amber. Amber was not happy about Cara finding me a new counselor.

"Look, sis, I'm not going to sign the consent form when Liam brings it to me. Cara works for that hospital. I'm going to tell him I'm not comfortable signing it because I am not sure if it is for a therapist or a psychiatrist. Our plan to lie to the counselor and have you tell them horror stories about Liam and Cara isn't going to work if the staff knows Cara. Anyone who knows her will know that it's all bullshit. It would be better for you to not even have a counselor than to see someone that might know Cara".

It's May, just 5 months before I turn 16. I start driver's training in 1 week. Being socially awkward and feeling like an outcast, Liam allowed me to sign up for virtual driver's training classes. I wouldn't have to worry about not knowing anyone in the class and he wouldn't have to worry about getting caught over at work and me missing a session. The school would be out in just 5 short weeks.

Amber had the baby, a little boy, Wyatt. She said it would be good for me to come and stay the entire summer with her. She said it would be good for me to start learning how to take care of a baby now because you never know when you might accidentally find yourself pregnant. I remember telling Layla I wanted to be a teen mom. That was when I was with Daniel. I thought maybe if I "accidentally" got pregnant, he would want to stay with me.

Lillian thought it was a terrible idea right away, but she was always the more cautious one of us. She said that most teen moms have to drop out of school to take care of the baby… and the guy ends up leaving them anyway. Layla thought it would be fun to have a little baby around, and we could all take turns holding it and playing with it. Having a baby seemed easy. You feed it, change it, and hold it. It just sleeps most of the time. I don't need training to take care of a baby.

Steve decided he was going to stick it out. He was trying to get close to me; he thought we could do some bonding. He talked to me every chance that he got. He said he could start giving me driving lessons and show me how to drive a stick shift (with a wink). He wants me to come live with him…and my mom. Says he would love to enjoy my company all summer long. He was always so nice to me. He told me I was beautiful. He agreed that I could have any guy I wanted, and he bet I would look great in a crop top and jean shorts with rips around the pockets.

Steve thinks my dad is too strict too. He says a young woman like me should be able to experiment and make my own grown-up decisions. He says I'm easy to talk to, not like my mother, and he enjoys the time we get to spend together alone. He offers to do the drop off, instead of my mom, when we switch for visitation. He likes being able to talk to me alone on the way to the carpool parking lot. It's nice that I understand him and don't treat him like "just some guy" my mom is dating. We could learn to be friends. If I came to stay with my mom, we could hang out more. He hopes that I want to spend more time with him. It would be nice to learn how to drive, so I told him I'd think about it.

Chapter Eighteen: Out of the Ashes

Meet Mitchell

Dakota has been getting on my nerves. I feel like she just wants there to be a problem in her life to compete with the problems that I have in mine. If I tell her my dad is being a dick, she tries to one-up me and tell me her dad is worse. If I tell her my dad yelled at me, she tells me her dad hit her. It's like she's starved for attention. She just wants me to like her. She tells me that she thinks I should date her cousin, Mitchell. She says he's kind of a bad boy and thinks I will like him. He's in my grade at my school. I have literally never heard of him. I'm leery about trying another guy she sets me up with. She has bad taste. The last time I dated someone she wanted me to, he spread rumors about me and him.

Then again, I really want a boyfriend. I'm tired of being a nobody. I go to her house to look up his Instagram together. She says that he is in a gang. Apparently, he smokes weed and runs the streets. While we are talking and stalking his Instagram, her dad pokes his head into the room. He says that he hopes that we're not talking about Mitchell. He tells me to avoid that kid that he's bad news. He says that the entire side of the family is bad news. Most of them are criminals and the other half just haven't been caught yet. Dakota tells her dad to mind his business. Initially, I was not attracted to him.

His face is kind of plain, and his nose is wide. He has long dark hair that falls to his shoulders. After hearing that he does whatever he wants, I find myself increasingly interested and attracted to him. I told Dakota to send my Instagram handle to him and my Snapchat.

It was awkward talking to him on FaceTime for the first time. I wasn't really sure what to say to him. We don't have anything in common. He told me that he thinks that I am beautiful, much prettier than his last girlfriend. I asked him who his last girlfriend was, and then I looked her up on Instagram. That's what we ended up talking about. I saw her picture and instantly felt jealous. I felt a claim to a boy that I'd only spoken to for 20 minutes. We basically bonded over me breaking down his girlfriend's appearance and telling him that he dodged a bullet by her breaking up with him.

After that one phone call, I was hooked. I spent the rest of the night going through his social media and "liking" all his photos. I told him that we should make this official and post that we were in a relationship with each other. We would only have three more weeks of school together. I am dreading summer vacation now. I definitely didn't want to go stay with my mom all summer. I just wanted to be with Mitchell now.

It had been two whole weeks. Mitchell was meeting me between classes and walking me to mine before he went to his. He was pulling chairs out for me so I could sit. He was walking me to the bus after school. I wanted everyone to see us together. I wanted everyone to see us hug and for him to kiss my cheek before I got on the bus. I wasn't a nobody. I was Mitchell's girlfriend. I felt like we had known each other so much longer than two weeks. We were great together. I told him that I loved him, and he said it back. This was the best thing that had happened to me in the last six months. I could feel that we were going to be together forever.

Things were not any better at home. I don't know why they would be. I had completely derailed from the tracks. I was throwing a temper tantrum over every little thing at home. If I was asked to do my chores, I threw a fit. I told Liam I didn't understand why Cara couldn't do it since she only works three days a week. She needed to be the one to pick up the slack. If I was asked to come down for dinner, I screamed at Liam that I hated him. I screamed that I hated everyone in the family and that I didn't want to eat with them. I threw a fit if he asked me to go to a movie, bowling, or to a restaurant for dinner. I told him that I am not part of this family and I have no interest and pretending to like people that I hate. Liam couldn't understand why I was so angry and lashing out all the time. He kept reiterating that nothing was going on in the house that should be making me this unhappy. He said that everyone in the household was working to make things better and I was the only one not putting in any effort.

Every time that I was disrespectful, Liam took my phone as

punishment. I was seething. How was I supposed to stay up talking to Mitchell until I fell asleep? How was I supposed to keep checking his location to make sure that he was really at home? He had already suggested that he wanted to go to a party at his friend's house. His ex-girlfriend was going to be there. They were probably just going to hang out and smoke. I could barely trust him, and now I couldn't even verify his whereabouts. I could just scream. Liam was ruining my life.

Now that it was June, I only had 2 weeks left of driver's training. How was he going to control me once I was able to drive? I could just grab my keys and leave, go wherever I wanted and come back whenever I felt like it. I would be in control of my own life. Why wait?

I would show him. He couldn't control me. I could do whatever I wanted. I could run away if I wanted. I could just go live with Mitchell. I didn't want to live with Liam anymore. I wanted to run away with Mitchell. If I left, there was nothing he could do to get me to come back home. Mitchell and I were in love, and we were already talking about getting married. I convinced Mitchell to have his sister pick us up from school instead of getting on the bus. I didn't ask permission, and I sure as shit did not tell anybody where I was going. He took my phone the night before, and I wasn't able to talk to Mitchell all night. He couldn't keep us apart. I felt like I could relate to Romeo and Juliet. He wouldn't be able to call me or track me without my phone.

His sister dropped us off at his uncle's house. We told her specifically not to tell anyone that they saw me. He told her he would pay her $20 for her discretion. His uncle lived in a trailer park not far from his house. We would just sit there and hang out with each other. We could be alone. We could make out. We could get to know each other better. Everything was going great (that may be an exaggeration) until Mitchell's mom called. He had shock and fear on his face. He even stepped out of the room to talk to her. When he came back, he told me that my dad had called the cops and they were on their way here; both the cops and my dad pick me up. I couldn't believe he had found me so quickly. His mom was pissed and threatened to beat him with a belt if he didn't tell her "where he was hiding that little white puta."

I begged him to leave his uncle's trailer with me. We could find another hideout. I told him that my dad was mean and abused me. I saw the look in his eye: concern…pity. He was fighting himself on what he should do. I told him that if we ran off, my mom would come pick me up. Anything would be better than going with my dad. I called my mom and told her I had run off with Mitchell. She already knew. My dad had already called her and my Grandma Amanda. I was going to be in deep shit for this. She asked me where I was and promised not to tell my dad. She also told me she was not going to come get me. The police were involved already, and she didn't want to be caught in the middle.

The police pulled up, Dad and Cara hot on his heels. Mitchell stayed inside and sent me out. I didn't know if he was watching from the window or not. I had never been in legal trouble before. I was trembling but trying to put on a brave, baddie face, just in case Mitchell could see me from the trailer. The officer explained that I was a child and had to return home with my dad. I told the cop I wasn't getting in my dad's Jeep. Surprisingly, he told me that I was, in fact, getting in that Jeep. He wasn't like the cop that sat around the school all day, goggling the moms and playing friends with the teens. He wasn't the one. I could either walk over and get in, or, he could put me in the Jeep, my choice.

There was no way that Liam was going to let this cop put his hands on me. So, I stood there, arms crossed. The officer gave me the "ok if that's what you want" look and snatched me up by the shoulders. Twisting and pushing me at the same time, he shoved me toward the Jeep. Stunned, I shuffled my awkward feet, half dragging the toes of my shoes into the gravel. His forearm and elbow were gouging me in the back. He threw open the backseat door, and I honestly thought he was going to potato sack me right into the seat, face smeared and abraded against the leather. I decided that I would just take an ungraceful squat into the seat before he had the chance. My ego was bruised and shriveling under his browed stare.

I did everything I could to regain control of the situation on the way home. First, I tried the silent treatment. Liam didn't deserve an answer. I would shun him for punishment. I didn't want to hear him speaking. See, Cara nodded her head in agreement while he denounced my plan as sporadic and unrealistic.

What exactly was your plan, huh? Were you just going to live at his uncle's house and then go to school from there every day? Was he going to come visit you after school? Were you just going to come home sometime in the night, and we would all pretend you hadn't been missing? How did you honestly see this playing out? Did you even think that far ahead? This is why children aren't allowed to make their own decisions. They live in spontaneous moments with no forethought of the long-term consequences of their actions. If you expect us to start treating you more adult like, you need to start making more responsible decisions.

The smug grin on Cara's face, like she couldn't be more proud of her puppy dog, set me off. "WHY IS SHE EVEN HERE! YOU AREN'T MY MOM"! If ostracism wasn't going to work, then I would gain control by being the loudest person in the Jeep. No one else would be able to speak over me. I called her every name except her own. I called her a bitch, cunt, and a slut. The trifecta. Why was she worried about me running around with boys? Didn't she get pregnant at 16? She was a slut. She should know what I planned on doing with him alone in the back bedroom of his uncle's house because she already lived the experience. How dare she look at me like I was dick crazed. That was rich coming from her. And do you know what that tyrant bitch said back? NOTHING. She just sat there quietly. I later found out that she promised my dad not to say anything or escalate the situation. I thought it was because I was getting to her. Really, it's because she was trying to bite her tongue out of respect for my father.

She didn't have to say anything anyway. Once I started verbally attacking Cara, my dad lost his shit instead. I am not exaggerating when I say the entire Jeep shook when he hollered at me to "shut my fucking mouth"! If he heard another disrespectful word, no, just any other word in general, he was going to punch me in the face. He slammed his balled-up fists against the steering wheel. I think the windshield was misted, with the spit coming off his lips. I had never seen him like this. This extreme. Of course, he was standing up for Cara. Choosing her over me. Reiterating that I was second rate, third rate if you counted Ella. Mitchell would never put me second.

Liam told me I could kiss that car goodbye. He wasn't giving me anything after that little stunt. I might as well quit driver's training, too. What was the point of learning to drive if I wasn't going to be getting the car? I hated him! My mom was right. He was only offering to give me the car, so he had something to take away from me. He enjoyed sucking the joy out of my life.

I wanted to call my mom. I wanted to hear what I wanted. She would tell me that it was fine that I had run off. She would say that hunting me down all day was exactly what Liam deserved. She would praise me for speaking to Cara the way I had. I didn't want to hear what a disappointment I had become anymore.

Judith had been helping him search the city for me. Ella was worried I had been kidnapped. Rachel, Judith's sister, had been praying for my safe return home. Zack made fun of me for trying to run away with a boy I had "just met." Amanda was frustrated with me. She couldn't believe I would do something so irrational. My Pa said I had a real problem with authority, and I needed to be put back in line. Judith begged my dad to let her come pick me up. She just wanted to take me out for ice cream and talk to me, you know, because "I had feelings too." My dad just hung up on her. That was one of the first times he had hung up on her for her absurd requests in what became a common occurrence over the next few months.

Everyone was turning on me. I had only three people left. Three people who would put up with my drama. One held on out of ignorance. He didn't know the truth, to know that I was lying. One held on out of pity and fear. Afraid that I would just let go of my will to live and end it all (even though at no point had I ever considered this). And the last one, well, she held on because, after all, we were shackled together. She wanted revenge. I was her outlet to hurt them. She wanted to control Liam through me.

Following my little incident, I went to my mom's for the weekend. As expected, she showered me with" good girl" treatment. I had earned her favor. If I played the game by her rules, she would let me do whatever I wanted. She was finally going to file the court petition for a change in custody. I was only four months away from being 16. The judge would definitely let me choose where I wanted to live. I would start by telling Liam I WAS going to be staying with her all summer. Then, she would make sure that Mitchell could come and stay the night or a few with me each week over the summer. Liam would never allow him to stay the night with me or vice versa. But Amber would.

It would be like living with him. All I had to do was write a letter to the judge. She sat me down and told me exactly what she wanted me to write. Once I was finished, she rewarded me with a new bikini. It was royal blue, 2-piece. The bottoms were a barely there cheeky cut with tie-string sides. The top was strappy triangle coverage with ties around my neck and chest. This is something Cara would never let me wear. I loved it! She understood me. She knew what was best for me. Letting me and Mitchell be together all summer was best.

When I got back to Liam's house, he told me that he was going to let me finish driver's training after all. I was almost finished. Then, if I could act right, he would let me sign up for segment 2. I wasn't going to play by his rules. I had new rules to follow, and I planned to adhere to these ones. I hadn't found my own voice. I found Amber's voice. I let it guide me through everything I did for the next four months. I basically told Liam to shove his reconsideration up his backside. I didn't care about driver's training, and I didn't care about losing that car. I don't care about anything. I don't need anything from him. I don't care about him or his money.

Amber was pleased to hear this. She encouraged it. As an award, she surprised me with a bundle of loose thong underwear. It was a little weird that she had picked out underwear for me, especially this kind, but I was still pleased. If I was going to have Mitchell around more, she thought I would want to be seen in something sexier. The thongs were exotic, to say the least.

They ranged from a burnt red lacey pair to a leopard-patterned pair. Most of them were outlined in lace, acting as a small peep show. There was a zebra-patterned pair. I don't know why animal skin is so sexy, but it just is. Then, there were ones with butterfly cutouts. A pink pair with the butterfly that sits above your butt crack. A black pair with a butterfly that sits over your vagina. I was glad she understood that Mitchell and I would be having sex while we lived with her. It would have been hard to sneak around with everyone that lives there.

She said not to worry about anything. If I came to live with her all summer, she would just put me back into driver's training, and at some point, she would make sure I got a car. I could get a job and work while I was there this summer to help pay her back for doing this for me. Not having a car put a little bump in our plans, but she was sure she could get my Grandma Amanda to drive me around. She would do this for me to get back at Liam. We wanted to get back at him.

Zack ended up getting in a nasty car accident. He had worked all day; then he went to help a friend with some demolition work for another 8 hours. He was driving home, almost made it, but ultimately fell asleep at the wheel. He woke up just in time to see he was headed head-on into a massive tree. He turned the wheel with microseconds to spare and crushed the passenger side. Totaled the car. Worst of all, he wasn't on a country road; he was in the city. The tree was placed in a family's front yard. If the tree hadn't smashed the car to a halt, their living room would have. He had minor bruises and a major adrenaline rush.

The officer responding was shocked to see him on the curb waiting. Literally asked him where the driver was. He was confused and admitted he was the driver. The officer said usually, when they pull up to a scene like this, the driver is dead. When the tow truck driver got there to yank the car back out of the tree, he said the same thing, the driver's normally dead.

Zack was lucky. Even luckier, my dad just happened to have

a car that he was getting rid of. My car. He offered it up to Zack to buy it off him, cheap. Without any other options, Zack took the keys and drove my dreams out of the driveway. That fueled my anger. Even after everything, I figured Liam would just give in and give me the car back. I hated being wrong.

Amber's promises made it easier for me to act psychotic at his house. The tantrums I threw were nothing short of a toddler missing a nap. I would scream and cry and hit my fists on the table. I made a point of telling him I hated him every day. When he tried to come to my room just to see me and ask me how my day was, I would scream at him to leave my room. Get out of my life. I hated him. Then, I would scream at him because he never gave me any attention.

I cried wolf to Judith now more than ever. We wanted her to believe I had never been happy at Liam's. I was always an outcast. I had never been comfortable. I told her that I was robbed of a mother. I never even had a mom to show me how to shave my legs (not that I needed one; women shave their legs in the movies. I'm not that dense). I didn't have a mother to show me how to stick a menstrual pad to the inside of my underwear (self-explanatory). I didn't feel comfortable asking Cara for anything, so I had to go my entire life with the bare minimum. I had to sit back and watch her give Ella everything. I couldn't even tell my dad how I felt because he never believed me. He was an absent father. It made her feel awful for me. She felt pity for me. She couldn't believe she was just, for the first time, finding out that I had lived in misery and solitude my entire life. How could she have never known?

Chapter Nineteen: Uno Reversing My Memories

Her Stories Suit Us Better

The more time I spent with my mom, the more stories about my father I heard. He was controlling and never let her do anything. He was jealous of her and was always worried that she would cheat on him because of how beautiful she was. So, at just 17 years old, he gave her an ultimatum to choose between him and her parents. He demanded that she move out and live with him so he could keep a better eye on her.

As foxy as she is now with her filtered picture in her Facebook profile, she claims that her beauty was undeniable when she was younger. Guys were chomping at the bit "to get her digits." My dad wouldn't allow her to work because he was worried that she would find another boyfriend, and he couldn't risk losing her. She was a great catch for someone like him. But he didn't treat her the way she deserved.

She was always so lonely. He wouldn't let her go out with her friends, but he would go out with his friends at the drop of a coin. Classic controlling behaviors. He would get to hang out with his family but didn't want her to spend time with her parents. He was slowly isolating her so he could have complete control over her. Her parents were so distraught when she left them, but they didn't fight her on it. At the time, she didn't realize what she was getting into; she didn't realize the kind of man he was.

He worked and used this as an excuse to be with other girls. He would pretend he was held over and would show up late at the house. She could smell other girls on him and knew in her heart that he was cheating on her, but she didn't have the strength to leave him. Not that he would have let her go.

When she did have enough courage to ask him about it, he would lie and become outraged. He smashed up things in their home. He broke lamps and shattered glasses. He punched holes in the drywall. He would scream at her until she cried and apologized to him. He would grab her and push her around, yank her off the couch even. She recalls a time she was so terrified that the only way she could get away from him was to stab him in the back with a pair of scissors. Everything after that fight was a blur.

She waited until he went to work about a week later, finally finding the courage and will to leave. She moved immediately in with another man, Roger, you know him. He was always the daddy when we played house. He would be able to protect her from my dad and his outburst of Narcissistic rage.

Nothing helped. He would drop by her new place and beg

her to take him back. She had left in such a hurry and accidentally took some of my father's things. Out of the kindness of her own heart, she offered to let him swing by to pick them up. He forced himself on her and pleaded with her. "One last time, for old times' sake"? A sort of proper goodbye. That's how she ended up pregnant with me.

As a matter of fact, he had pleaded with her to have an abortion shortly after he discovered the pregnancy. She had to tell him that she was pregnant with Roger's baby so he would drop it. He didn't want me from the moment they conceived me. He was disgusted with the idea of her having his baby and thought, "The baby would just turn out to be trash, just like her." He was more than willing to just let Roger father me. After all, she had already put Roger's name on my birth certificate anyway, and it was going to be a pain to have it corrected for her "little mix-up."

After she had me, she used to ask Liam if he wanted to see me all the time, but Cara didn't want to have me around. He already had Zack and was content with a son. He never wanted a daughter. Especially a daughter with her. If he couldn't have her, he didn't want a constant reminder of what he was missing out on.

She didn't just have stories about Liam. She told me things about Cara, too. She told me that Cara couldn't stand Liam coming to get me from my mother because he was thinking about leaving her and getting back with my mother when I was an infant. She was always so jealous of my mother.

When Zack was younger, Cara was such a bad parent CPS had to take him from her. She had to give her parents temporary custody of him while she went to parenting classes. She was very neglectful. She would leave Zack in soiled diapers and forget to buy formula to feed him.

She told me that Cara barely made it through nursing school. She basically had to cheat at the end to get by. They felt bad for her the last few semesters because she was pregnant, so they were going easy on her. When she had Ella, they simply passed her because she was a new mom and couldn't study or go to clinics.

She let me know Cara used to be mean to me whenever Liam wasn't around. She would taunt me and even hit me. I never told Liam in these stories, but I would come home from the weekend. I was only 2 years old, and I would tell my mother everything terrible she had done to me over the weekend. Cara would wipe boogers on the walls in my room and blame it on me, so Liam would make me clean it up. She was always a real monster.

According to my mom, Judith always called her, especially in the beginning, because she wanted her to take Liam back. Judith was always fearful for me. Cara was abusive and would belittle Liam and even smack him from time to time. That's why he was always doing what Cara wanted. Not because he wanted to but because he was scared of her. Also, Judith says she thinks Cara is secretly a lesbian. She always hangs out with her friends, going on girl's trips. They have too intimate of a relationship to be just friends. Judith told my mom she had always wished my dad would leave Cara.

The thing is, I don't remember any of this. Obviously, I wouldn't know anything about their relationship before I was born. During our arguments, I bring up bits and pieces of these stories and the others she told me, and Liam completely denies it. He tells me that my mother is making up stories. He says she's batshit crazy and delusional.

According to Liam, the only part of her entire story that was true was that she definitely stabbed him in the back with scissors (and not because she was defending herself). She also hit him with her car. He says that she was very young and very jealous. He says it sounds like she is telling stories about herself but substituting his name. He also implied that my mother was a whore, and that is why she didn't know who fathered her kid.

He also says that he never asked my mother to have an abortion. He claims he didn't even know she was pregnant for a long time. She called him up after I was born and told him she thought I was his. He said if he never wanted me, he wouldn't have agreed to take a paternity test. He said he was trying to do the right thing and stepping up to be my father…look where that has gotten him.

He says he doesn't know what she is on, but "it must be some good shit" because not a single thing she said about Cara is true. I don't understand why she would just make up all these elaborate stories to tell me. He says, "With her, he's not surprised by anything anymore". He says he'll tell me if I want to hear true stories about my mom and him. He says things weren't always bad, and they didn't always hate each other. He says at one point, a long time ago, he did think he loved her. He said he remembers her making him buy her promise ring. He says he should have known better because it didn't feel right even when he gave it to her. Sometimes, two people aren't necessarily bad people. They just aren't the right people for each other. He says she's changed a lot from when they were together.

It's really a lot of "he said, she said crap." It's confusing me. The way my mother tells a story, she's always the victim. She has always tried to do the right thing or was the bigger person. This doesn't exactly match up with her behaviors over the years. No matter how shitty she makes Liam out to be, he just has never been that way. It's not like a narcissist would just get better. Why isn't he that person when he is with Cara? If her stories are true, she must have brought out the worst in him.

The way she describes Cara doesn't feel right. I vaguely remember being happy when I was with her as a small child. Dancing with me, reading to me. She used to make my birthday cakes herself (she was a cake decorator before she was a nurse). I can look in the photo albums and see that I was smiling, laughing even. I wasn't stuck to Liam's side; I was usually in her embrace. She helped me pick out the dresses I wore. She brushed and styled my hair. She went to dances with me. She made me special.

I don't know who to believe. Liam doesn't seem like he is lying. He always seems genuine when he answers my questions or talks to me. He offered to let me read the CPS reports outlining the investigations of my graphic childhood leading up to her losing custody. She says he's blowing "smoke up my skirt," and there are no reports. He offered to pull up his account online to see all the child support payments he did indeed make, the ones Amber says he never did. I want to believe my mother, though. Besides, it will be easier to hate Liam when I go to live with her if I pretend these stories are true, even if they are only true in my head.

Learning to despise Ella will make it easier to leave her, my childhood friend. For a long time, my bedtime protector. My anger for her comes so easily. Walking home from school, she got a phone call. Someone wanting to hang out with her later. When I asked her who it was, she replied, Lillian. Why do the Ls still want to be her friend when they refuse to be mine? After all the trouble I went through to try to keep them apart. I worked so hard for them to like me, to be friends with me alone. It appears the tables have turned, and I am distraught. I am unstable. I do not take rejection well.

I lash out at Ella. I tell her Lillian is not welcome at MY house. Ella has the audacity to tell me that it isn't my house. Like the child she is, she tells me it's our parents' house. She can have any friend over that she wants.

Furthermore, she sourly reminds me that when Layla and she weren't getting along, I made sure to still have her over. Who does she think she is? Just because I did something in the past, she thinks she has the right to do the same thing.

I can't let it go. Cara is at work, and Dad has been mandated. Perfect. I keep verbally stabbing her. She's a selfish brat. She's a mama's girl. She's fat. I can tell she is trying to ignore me. I keep coming downstairs to keep the attacks coming. It's the most I've been downstairs this whole week. I pretend to be on the phone, laughing and making fun of her. I tell my invisible friend on the other end that she's a selfish snot. She has no friends of her own, so she has to take my sloppy seconds. She asks me who I am talking to. None of her business. That's who. She can sulk over my disgruntled comments for the rest of the night for all I care. Looking back, I feel like I was unconsciously creating a mutual hate to make things easier to leave for me and her.

Leftovers

Without a doubt, Ella snitched on me to Cara. When I hear Cara pull into the driveway, I jump into my bed and start to pretend to sleep. I can dish it out but I don't want to take it from Cara tonight. Karma brings the soft knuckle raps against my door. She comes into my room, leaving my light off. She calls out my name. She's persistent. She's not leaving. She asked me about what happened today. She wondered if maybe something happened at school to put me in a bad mood. She tells me what she's already heard from Ella. Oddly, she isn't chastising me. She sounds concerned. She asks what happened between Lillian and me why am I so upset with her? Is she bothering or harassing me? Does she need to speak to her father?

Somehow, here I am, spilling my heart out to her again. It's like a spell she has over me. "I feel like I have to compete with Ella." She tells me it's nonsense. Both of us matter in this house. She loves both of us, and it's not about taking sides. She wants to know if I am having problems, if I am struggling. She can help me if I let her. She offers to finish the laundry I left in the washer, kisses my forehead, and leaves my room. That was not the interaction I was expecting. It's not the interaction I deserved.

Cara is a nurse. Stereotypically, that means she is caring and nurturing. More than that, she's a problem solver. She wants to cure people. She wants to heal me. She can sense my hurt and just wants to fix it and make it disappear.

She must have been thinking about my vulnerability last night all day. When I came home, I found another letter sitting on my dresser.

Ava,

I hope you understand that I will always choose you at the end of the day. You matter to me. When you hurt, I feel it. I know sometimes you can't tell, but every choice I make is with you in mind. I have chosen you every day since I knew you existed, and I will choose you even when you want me to let go.

When your dad first told me about you, I was excited to meet you. I chose you. I could have walked away. I didn't have to stay, but I wanted to. I chose you. I chose to care for you, sing to you, rock you to sleep while you screamed inconsolably into my ear.

When we learned about the terrible things you were living through, I chose you. I chose to help your father. I chose to write out your father's court documents and appeals. I chose to keep fighting for you because you matter. You are not just his daughter. You are mine.

I chose to raise you. I chose to do all the things required to raise a young girl and all the things to make her childhood special for you. I chose to be involved in every activity you wanted to try, in every sport. I chose to show up and support you. I chose to run you around to all your games, meetings, and activities. I chose to go on your field trips, not because I wanted to chaperone a bunch of children, but because I chose you.

When I check in on your grades, it's not to hassle you. It's because I know you are capable. I want you to have all the best opportunities. I want to prevent challenges. I wish I could be your friend all the time, but I sometimes have to be a parent. I promise it's because I am choosing to believe in your future.

Hearing that you feel unloved kills me. It kills me because I have chosen you every day for almost 16 years. I have chosen to love you. I have chosen to support you and guide you. I have chosen to hop through hoops and to keep doing my best. I have chosen to reflect on my words and actions and chose to try to be better- for you.

I may not have given birth to you, but you are MY daughter. You have never been second. The Montana mountainside and a field of Monarchs are both amazing and beautiful. They are entirely different, but nevertheless, outstanding and unique in their own way. That is how I feel about you and Ella, equally amazing. I chose you, then. I choose you now. Even when you push me away, I choose you. I love you. You matter to me. I see you.

Love now and always,

Cara

Chapter Twenty: Blood, Shit, and Tears

Revenge Plans Wasted

I know what she has written is true. I'm upset. I'm not upset with her for pointing out all the things she has done for me over the last few years. I'm upset because my mother would not do those things for me. This letter reminded me that Amber had never chosen me. Cara is right, and she didn't have to choose me. She didn't have to step up as a mom just because mine wouldn't. My mom didn't want Cara to replace her, but she just couldn't find it in herself to be there for me when it really mattered. I don't like being sad about my mom. I usually pretend that she did the best she could. She's here for me now, though, right?

School is wrapping up this week, and my dad has been on me for days. I've made flashcards, and he's been making me sit at the table and repeat the answers back to him. He's asked about study guides and phoning friends to help find the answers to the guide. I can't afford to fail the final exam in Biology. I had been skipping it so much to hang out with the counselor that this would be my last shot at passing the class. I have to pass this test, or I am re-doing Biology next year. I should have stopped going down there, especially once Mitchell and I started dating. It was awkward to talk about Daniel and moving forward when all I was focused on now was Mitchell and my relationship.

During an assembly about a month ago, I asked my dad to come to pick me up because I didn't have any friends to sit with now that the L's and I were done, and I wasn't sure where Dakota was. One of the guys I used to talk to told me I could come sit by him, but then he was just letting me so he could embarrass me in front of his friends. I was mortified. I ran down to the office and called my dad. He told me, "I can't keep running from my problems." He was not going to come get me. "I needed to put my big girl panties on and find somewhere else to sit." The counselor was on the speaker phone with us and heard him say that. She's *sensitive,* to put it mildly. She apologized to me for my dad saying that. That's when I figured she would suffice for what my mom was trying to accomplish. She wanted a counselor on her side when she went to court to paint my father as a "cold and heartless father." She wanted her to vomit up all the lies I was supposed to be telling her about all year for the judge when asked.

I was trying to get all the stars aligned, just so, as my mom asked. I had written the letter she asked for. I had flipped Judith back to our side. I had manipulated and distorted my reality for the school counselor. I had thrown tantrums for Liam. I was working on cutting ties with everyone else. It was going to be just Mitchell, and I left to support each other. We were all we needed for each other. By senior year, I imagined he would propose after spending the entire summer with me. Directly after high school, we would be wed. I would still technically be a minor, but because my mom would be winning custody soon, she would just sign off for us to be married underage. By 18, maybe sooner, we would be starting our own family. I was hoping to be pregnant before long. If I had his baby growing inside of me, he would never leave. I wouldn't have to worry. Between our moms, we could have plenty of people to help us with the baby.

I had been planning everything perfectly, and then Liam dropped a bomb on my world. He told me I would not live with my mother all summer. He said that he never agreed to that. I tried to argue with him that he told me I could. He was ruining everything. He was ruining my life. I tried making him feel guilty. I tried making him angry. I tried telling him that just because he forces me to stay with him won't make me love him. It will just make me hate him more and lose respect for him. He said, "That's fine. I guess we will be exactly where we are now then".

We had problems that needed to be dealt with. I needed to work on rebuilding bonds with this family, too. Just because I wanted to rekindle a relationship with my mom didn't mean I had to sabotage the ones I had here.

He agreed to let me go to my mother's every other week. He considered it a fair compromise because he didn't have to agree. Pissed, I told him that I would be staying the week with my mom right off the get-go instead of just the weekend. My plan was once I was there to just beg and beg him to let me stay until he eventually changed his mind.

As pattern would have it, my mother also betrayed me. I had made all these plans for the summer. I was going to have Mitchell live with us all summer, get a job, get back into driver's training, and by the time summer ended, my mother would have custody, and I wouldn't even have to worry about going back to his house. Except, now she is telling me that we are going to be camping all summer in a popup camper by the Hoosier National Forest. That is almost 3.5 hours away from South Bend.

There aren't going to be any jobs for me there. There isn't going to be internet access or Wi-Fi at this campground. How will I be joining virtual driver's education without reliable internet service? Mitchell didn't have a car. Not to mention, he already had a job at Perkins as a dishwasher/busboy. That was too far of a drive for him. His sister sometimes gives him a lift because his mom doesn't drive, but there is no way she will drive him this far. It's like she promises me one thing and then proceeds to do the exact opposite.

I could lose my mind if I hadn't already lost it. I hate camping. The campground is boring. It's just empty lots, scraggly trees, and kiddie playgrounds. There isn't even a community pool.

This campground is definitely for old people who just like to people watch outdoors. Worse, my grandparents aren't even coming. It's just my mom, Steve, and my three siblings. The baby cries all the time, and we all have to be bunched together in a small Coleman popup camper.

There is a small pond to fish in. Steve brought poles. At least I have my new bikini. I can try to get a tan if I am going to be trapped here for the whole week. I can go swimming with Trudy. She's not as close to my age as Ella is, but she'll do. I hate to admit that I wish Ella was here. I just have more in common with Ella. We have more to talk about because we have the most memories together…that thought alone makes me sad. I get a nauseating feeling that I am making a mistake.

Another mistake I made was thinking that eating gas station biscuits and sausage gravy was a good idea. I had left it out in the car and forgot to get it in the fridge when we returned to the campground. My mom was having cigarettes for breakfast, and I had to have those damn biscuits. When I finally reheated them for lunch, I should have known. The worst part about it was I had started wearing those thong underwear my mom gifted me earlier. I wanted to break them in and get used to anal chaffing before Mitchell saw me in them for the first time. There was no material. There was nothing to catch the loads and splatters of diarrhea that ricocheted off my butt cheeks and plastered my legs, streaming to my ankles. I ruined three pairs of thongs that day alone. Never believe a fart is just a fart when you have diarrhea. These farts burned your butthole on the way out and soiled the 1cm strip of fabric wedged in between your ass cheeks.

Mistake number three: track your period. Just when I thought it couldn't get worse. The diarrhea finally drizzled its last drops, but then the river of red consumed what was left of my thongs. It never occurred to me that there was no graceful or tactful way to strap a pad to a thong. It either had no material to stick to and adhered to my leg, leaving my underwear in pure carnage, or it became stuck to itself like a tourniquet around the crotch, and I had to rip through the bloody pad with the force of a warrior to get it back off and smeared blood everywhere. Obviously, there were no laundromats around here. I would just shove them into my backpack and pray the smell didn't attract the wildlife in my sleep.

At the end of the weekend, I call my dad and beg him to come home. I don't want to stay here for the whole week. He has been mandated and cannot come until the next day to pick me up. I feel disgusting in my own skin. I haven't bathed in 3 days. My legs have a brown tinge to them from the aforementioned accidents. The bathrooms are run down. I don't have a razor to shave my legs. Not to mention, I didn't bring a toothbrush. I thought I would be going to my grandma Amanada's or my mom's house. I wasn't planning on camping, and I didn't pack accordingly.

My phone did get a little service. I played games on it most of the time. My sister and brother are annoying. Issac was out of control. My mom lets him listen to rap music; his swearing is worse than mine. He's only 3 years old. He has been running around unbridled for 3 days now, bullying other little kids at the campground and cussing at even adults. He's been doing this vulgar hand gesture where he only puts out his second, third, and pinky finger and yells, "Two in the pink and one in the stink." I feel embarrassed when the parents look at our campsite with mortified expressions.

When my dad met us, I was relieved. I am so looking forward to a shower. I tell him how disgusting the campground is. I tell him that I have changed my mind and there is no way I can live there all summer. As a matter of fact, I tell him that I don't even want to go back next week. He laughs and says, "That didn't last long". I'm a little perturbed because I feel like he knew this was going to happen. I missed being in my own room, with my own bed, with a door that locks. I can have some privacy for the first time in 4 days. I can finally talk to Mitchell the way I want without having Trudy or Issac come bursting into the camper when I tell them to leave me alone.

I am disheartened to hear that Mitchell wasn't really planning on staying with my mom and me this summer anyway. He says with school being out, he can pick up the most hours at work. I jokingly tell him if he's making all that money, he should buy me a ring. Once I've said it, I can't get the idea out of my head. We have been dating for about 4 weeks now and are serious. I don't correct him when he asks if I mean a promise ring. Any ring will do at this point. I need to have something that proves that we belong to each other. I want to make sure everyone else knows. I push the issue for the whole night until he finally agrees that he will try to save some money to buy me one. Before the call ended, I was already looking at ring size measuring gauges on Amazon.

Even after Liam came to pick me up almost a week early, strictly as a favor, I still treated him poorly. He has to ride me to do my chores, and I give him shit until he threatens to take my phone again. I tell him this is exactly why I hate him. I tell him that he needs to earn my respect and that making me clean up after HIS family is not the way to earn my respect.

I was lying around in my room watching Netflix when Mitchell surprised me and asked me to go to the movies with him. This was going to be interesting. I just told Liam off, and now I was going to have to tuck my tail and ask him to give me a ride to and from the movies. UGH. It'll be fine, though. *It doesn't matter how terrible I am. He'll always forgive me.*

And he did.

Like a boomerang, I managed to go back to visit with my

mom. Seeing Mitchell at the movies and having the constraints of not being alone with privacy, just in the dark of the crowded theater, made me revisit the plot my mother was planning. My dad was never going to let me be truly alone with him. I was hoping by now, I could have pledged my eternal love to Mitchell by giving him all of me. I wanted him to take my virginity. I wanted him to be my first. If I did this, he would know how much I loved him, and he would want to stay with me forever.

I had to increase my attitude tenfold. I had to start throwing bigger fits. I had to express my anger and hatred in the most obnoxious ways possible. I had to learn not to enjoy a moment in his home. Even more, I had to make sure anyone who would listen understood how unimaginably miserable I was.

What would have been game face time, turned out to have a small bump in the road. Due to unforeseeable circumstances, I had to call my dad and play nicely. While I was being bothered and pestered to spend time with Trudy, I begrudgingly went out on the lake in a small pedal boat with her. I made her do all the work while I played free downloaded games on my phone. Hearing her badgering me to "please pedal" was so annoying. I didn't even want to be out here on this lake. I wanted to be with Mitchell. Why couldn't anyone understand that he was the only person that mattered in my world?

She must have gotten sick and tired of doing all the work because she was pedaling us back to the dock. I was mid-selfie when she shook the boat, trying to wriggle herself onto the dock. I told her to wait a minute for me to take the picture. I wanted Mitchell to believe that I was having the best summer. I mean, that's what social media is all about creating these perfect personas to make others envious of life you aren't truly even living. Anyway, she kept rocking that damn boat until I slipped, jostled, and my phone slipped straight out of my finger grip, sinking immediately to the bottom of that damn lake.

Cue the screaming, tears, threats, and tantrums. The only thing I loved more than Mitchell was my phone, which was now "swimming with the fish." Even if I deployed the emergency dive team to retrieve my beloved, it would be ruined. It wasn't waterproof. It was a goner. My mother said I should be more responsible and there was no chance of her buying me a new phone. She started to ask why you think we are camping all…and Steve cut her off. If I was going to get a new phone, I was going to have to call up my arch-enemy, my father.

I was surprised he answered when I called him from my mother's phone. I started by buttering him up right away. I told him I called him because I missed him and just wanted to tell him I loved him. He responded with, "You must want something". I told him that my phone had fallen into the lake, and I needed him to buy me a new one. I told him that he could head up and pick me up earlier and go to the store to pick it out when we got home. He told me, "Nice try," and he did not come to get me earlier just to buy me a phone, especially the way I have been treating him lately.

This is exactly why I hate him. He treats me like he doesn't owe me everything. I didn't ask to be born. He wanted me to be here, so he should be providing me with everything I need to make me happy. My behavior shouldn't dictate whether he buys me things or not. He says he'll get me a phone, but I have to wait. I need to earn it, and prove that I can act right before he just buys me one. The audacity he has.

Once my grandparents visited, my Pa told me a buddy had a phone he was not using at his campsite. He talked him into letting me have it. It's an older Android phone, but I'll take it. An older phone is better than no phone. It only has a few games on it and no service yet. As I surf through it, I find that it isn't wiped clean. It still has all his contacts in it. It still has a full gallery. He has so many photos of fish. There are a few hunting photos and dead deer. Old people take photos of the weirdest things.

There are a few video files. These are not dead animals and fish. These are all pornographic. There are some downloaded videos of random strangers licking each other's asses. Then, there are some "homemade" videos of him stroking his geriatric dick. I'm both disgusted and intrigued. It's like a car crash; you know you will see something bad that you may never forget, but at the same time, you can't look away.

I have had this phone for almost two weeks. I don't immediately delete these files. I watch them repeatedly. I don't know how they make me feel. The taboo of me watching something forbidden and unintended for me makes me feel excited. Instead of deleting them, I tell my Grandma Amanda about the videos and tell him what a creep their friend is. My Pa took the phone. He doesn't delete the videos and give it back. He takes it, upset, and returns it to his friend. He tells him that his minor granddaughter inadvertently came across his porn. Even though he was doing me a favor, my Pa says he should have cleared the phone before he gave it to a child. And now, I'm phoneless again.

Sometime in between visits, my dad told me that my mom spoke to him and felt that I should be put on birth control. It felt like a small betrayal. I'm not sure why she would disclose something like that to him. I wanted, no NEEDED, to get pregnant with Mitchell's baby. Why couldn't anyone understand? I told him I would take the pill (even though I planned on just throwing them away and not actually taking them), but I didn't want him to tell the doctor why I needed them. We decided that I would complain of irregular periods and painful cramps.

The first day we got them, he watched me take the first pill. It felt like scratchy defeat sliding down my throat. I didn't want anything to do with these pills. I have never been able to swallow pills, so he wanted to make sure that I could take them. After I proved I could, he handed me the pack to take to the campground. He also gave me a new iphone, kind of. It was Cara's, but she got a new one and gave me hers. It was in mint condition, wiped clean, and back to the factory setting, with a new case. I threw a stink about him not getting me a brand-new in-the-box phone. However, later, I texted Cara that I really appreciated her getting me the phone. I don't know why I can't just show him a single strand of gratitude.

Once I was back at my mother's campsite, I pitched that pack immediately. I may have taken one, but there was no way anyone was getting me to take a single other one of the twenty-seven remaining tablets. It was my mom's idea to have them prescribed, and I know my dad told her about them, but she didn't ask me once about the pills, so I made sure to not bring up anything about my appointment, the pack, or the one pill I did take.

My mom started keeping track of all the terrible interactions I was causing between my father and me. She congratulated me on my efforts. She said it was going to be a "walk in the park" getting custody at this point. She asked me about Judith and if I felt like she was on our side. She was planning on having her act as a witness and needed her primed with all these stories and problems before the court. That I could do; she was very easy to manipulate, especially when she thought she would be declared one of the heroes in my story.

Judith is actually where I got my next best plan. Just in case the court didn't go my mom's way, I'd have a plan B. Judith told me when I turned 16 that I could just get emancipated, and then I could just move out of my dad's. I am positive she meant I could leave and then just come live with her, the hero, but I had other ideas. I would move in with Mitchell and his mom. It seemed like either way, I was going to get what I wanted. I knew there would be no problem with us staying with my mom or Grandma Amanda, but I wasn't quite sure if his mom would let me move in. If I was pregnant, she probably would, though. People feel bad, pity if you will, for young teen moms.

Just as the summer was meeting its halfway point, my dad surprised me yet again with a new counselor. He said I should be happier because she is young and a female, just like I asked. Apparently, I had been on this waiting list for almost two years, and she finally had an opening. Yeah, for me (I hope you can sense the sarcasm). Cara took me to my first appointment. She sat in the lobby, and I went back alone. This was exactly the way I wanted it. I also quickly realized that, unlike my last counselor, Liam and Cara had not spoken to her beforehand, so she wouldn't realize or understand what was really going on at home. She would be easy to manipulate, which would make Amber happy.

After a few sessions, it felt like things were going great. Meaning I had successfully told her that the only good relationship in my life was the one I had with Mitchell and my mother. I was getting great at playing the victim. I was asking her how one gets custody if they can't afford a lawyer. My mother specifically asked me to ask her that. It seemed she was having a difficult time coming up with the money to secure a lawyer. Brittany readily answered all my questions.

After feeling confident in my manipulative skills, Cara pulled the rug out from beneath my feet as we were leaving. She called Brittany back to the door I had just exited and asked her about my next appointment. I almost stopped listening to the mundane conversation, but then I saw Cara hand some papers over to her and comment, "Liam said it would be fine to give these to you. You don't have to look at them right now. These are just some concerns we have". ALWAYS intervening. She ruins everything. I wanted so desperately to know what was written on those papers. I wouldn't let my vulnerability and anxiety show, though. I wasn't going to ask, even though it was eating me alive to know.

It must have been something very intriguing because Brittany contacted my father and asked to speak with him privately before my next session. She had a few "questions". After all, except

10 minutes of *my* appointment were up, he came strolling out, shit-eating grin on his face, laughing away. Instantly pissed me off. They were clearly getting along, and she was no longer under my spell. I couldn't help myself. I called out, "Why is he laughing"? Brittany dismissed it, saying they had a good session, and then called me back for a few minutes. She wouldn't disclose anything they talked about to me. I could only let my mind create its own various explanations of what was discussed. Each made me the fool and him the tall, dark, and funny guy she loved to chat with.

I know it had something to do with my mom. I don't know why he couldn't just drop it. She wasn't very good at being a mom when I was young. But she had changed. She was better now, and she wanted to be my mom again. Cara has brainwashed everyone into thinking there is something wrong with me because of Amber. It's not true. Nothing that happened to me when I was younger even bothers me now. It has not affected me in any way. She thinks she knows everything, but she doesn't. She just doesn't want to see me happy. She's the big bad wolf my mom warned me about. The sheep wool is just slipping down now, so you can see her wolf fur better.

My mom is, of course, not happy to hear that Brittany is asking me questions about her now. Asking me questions about how certain events made me feel. She is no longer focused on Liam and Cara. She is focused on Amber. I wouldn't go as far as to say she doesn't think I am a victim. It's clear that she does. She has an undeniable look of pity for me just beneath the surface of her stare.

She thinks I am a victim, alright. I get the feeling she believes my mom is the perpetrator now…and the many boyfriends she has exposed me to over the years.

Amber called my dad and got Brittany's information. Fruitless. She said that that snot nose counselor was "so far up my dad's ass now" that she wouldn't even talk to her on the phone. Something about patient confidentiality. Amber says we have to ditch her. She won't be of any help at court like she had been hoping. We are going to have to rely on the school counselor, after all.

I'm infuriated with Liam. I spent all those sessions reliving a reality I created to get her on our side, and within one session, he had ruined everything. I screamed at him that he was a liar. He had either said he was a good parent or he said he was a bad parent who wanted to be better. Either way, he ruined counseling for me. It was never about "getting better". It was strictly about getting back at him. It was about revenge for my mother. Revenge for taking me in the first place. Revenge for not letting me wear those God damn crop tops. Revenge for taking Cara's side instead of mine. Revenge for loving Ella instead of just me. Revenge for taking my phone. Revenge for not letting me have sex with Mitchell. He was standing in the way of my ultimate happiness. He deserved to pay.

Chapter Twenty-One: Slapped with Reality

The Anticipation of Court

Cara had planned a trip for us, not too far from home, just to Ohio. We would stay in Mason. It was close to Cincinnati, and she had planned to let us go shopping at the outlet malls there. We might go to the zoo. The Airbnb had its own private pool, but she had planned it here because it was close to King's Island. We had never been there, and I specifically told her I wanted to go "somewhere with an amusement park." Cedar Point was closed the week we were going in preparation for the off-season.

That is the thing about Cara, the thing I just can't fault her for. It's hard to be truly angry with her when she does things like this. She makes sure that she plans everything accordingly. Each trip is special to make everyone happy. Ella wants to shop. Liam wants to relax and eat food not readily available at home. She wants to relax and read. I want to go to an amusement park…and voila, she makes it happen. We can't go very far because Dad only has one week off, and he wants to come back early because he has an annual man trip that weekend. Because there was a pool that had to be private, she went out and bought us girls all new bathing suits. She even bought us these ridiculous oversized hats. Why is it so hard to hate her?

I put up a front and acted like I didn't want to go. I intentionally waited until the last moment to pack. I didn't talk to anyone on the way down and refused to speak at lunch. They gave us spending money and took us to the outlets. They took us to lunches and dinner and the Cheesecake Factory, which I love. Dad even let me choose some of the restaurants we ate at. We swam in the pool and took selfies in our hats. Liam played PIG with me in the pool, and Cara convinced me to go down the sketchy slide. We all sat around, laughed, and played card games. We took turns listening to songs. We laughed as Liam ate gummies that had, unknowingly, been not only on the floor but on Ella's feet. Cara got us to play jokes on Liam, and we all nonchalantly took his basketball shorts out of his luggage, put them on and came down the stairs one by one wearing them, acting like nothing was going on. I wanted to hate the trip, for Amber's sake. I wanted to feel like the unwanted black sheep of the family.

Even King's Island was great. Cara normally doesn't like roller coasters, but she decided to come out of her comfort zone and ride anyway. I rode with Dad, and she rode with Ella. There were some rides we couldn't get on because, for some reason, Liam wouldn't just rent a locker for her backpack. If they wouldn't allow her to have the bag, we didn't ride on the coaster. She would have easily just waited and let us ride. I was secretly glad because some of the rides made me nervous. I was scared to ride a lot of the rides and was glad to see they were down at the moment, or we skipped them over because of the backpack. Even while we walked from gift shop to gift shop, allowing me to search for the perfect souvenir, I wanted to hate this trip. I felt guilty for having a good time when I knew Amber would want the opposite.

We returned home to Indiana merely weeks before school was to start. Everyone was preparing things and tidying up loose ends before school was to start. I may have forgotten to mention that Liam and Cara quickly learned I never took the birth control as planned. It was not a reasonable option for me. The next step was to have the contraception either injected or implanted. I chose to have the implant in my arm.

The Friday before school was to start, Cara had me scheduled for insertion. Dad was working, so Cara took me to the appointment. Honestly, I was glad it was her and not him. Whether I like to admit it or not, she has a very calming energy. I felt safe with her. She explained everything to me before the doctor came in. She held my hand through the procedure, and I didn't have to feel embarrassed to squeeze her hand. She squeezed mine while the doctor numbed my skin. She took down all the important aftercare instructions. While I was relieved to have her comfort me, I was also sad. Getting pregnant was not going to happen so long as this was in my arm.

The next trip was a last-minute decision. Cara and Liam just so happened to both have Labor Day Weekend off, so we were going to go camping and Razor riding. This time, I threw an actual temper tantrum. I was crying and screaming. Screaming that I was NOT going. Liam said I could either walk to the truck or he would place me in the truck. It was not an option to stay. I was crying and stuttering. Snot was running down my face. I told him if he made me go, I was going to make his whole trip bad. I was going to be terrible if he made me go. He wouldn't budge. I tried begging him to let me stay with Judith. It wasn't going to happen.

My mom said she finally filed the court papers, and this was it…the final countdown, if you would. She filed for an emergency hearing to have the judge decide whether there should be a change in custody. Ultimately, she could not afford the lawyer. An emergency petition was her only option. There was no room for turning back. I needed to cut ties with Liam, Cara, and Ella. I needed to get prepared to move out of their house and into Amber's house.

I kept my promise and it was absolutely absurd the entire time. I threw a fit about being there. I threw a fit about sharing a room with Ella. I threw a fit about having to eat lunch. I threw a fit about going into the store to pick out my own snacks. I absolutely refused to go riding with Cara and Liam. And do you know what they did? They just kept the trip going, kept offering me things, and kept trying to have a civilized conversation with me. At lunch, Cara asked me about my plans for the next semester. Talked to me about my plans after high school. Offered to help me figure things out. These people just can't seem to take a hint that I want to hate them.

The day they were heading over to the dunes to ride, I chose to pick a fight with Ella. Fighting with them and insulting my dad wasn't getting me anywhere. I needed a different angle to get under their skin. I wanted to stay back from the ride, lay around and talk to Mitchell. My service was shotty, but I needed to hear him; have him reassure me that I wasn't the problem. I was perfect. Then I found out Ella was also going to stay back, and I was enraged. Why did she get to stay back?

Liam said I was acting crazy. "What made me think I was better than everyone else? What made me think that I got to do whatever I wanted and got to decide what others did"? He said if I didn't knock my attitude off, he would let Ella stay back, and he would make me go. I knew not to call his bluff, so I restrained myself for a few hours.

By bedtime, I was in deep conversation with Mitchell. I was neck-deep in victimhood. Ella came in to go to bed, and I was obligated to start raising hell. Full-blown bitch mode, if you will. I came storming out of our room, not expecting to see Liam standing right there after I had just threatened Ella. Rather than cowering, she laughed and mocked me instead. Immediately, my phone privileges were in jeopardy again. I tried leaving the house, Liam grabbed the back of my sweater and told me to have a seat on the couch. He told me he had had enough. He was over this new entitled me. Cara came out of the room and just seeing her face made me angry. There was no getting away with anything when she was around. He didn't back down when she was his audience.

Cara looked down at her phone during my tantrum. I suddenly felt overwhelmingly paranoid that she was recording me. I felt like she was going to blackmail me. She was going to threaten to show everyone the real me instead of the victim I told everyone I was. I accused her of recording me. I accused her of wanting to blackmail me. I immediately changed my behavior. I stopped screaming and started listening. In a nutshell, Liam told me he wants me to be happy at both his house and my mom's. He wants what is best for me. He wants me to be successful. Everyone in the house loves me and wants me to get help to be better.

Afterward, I took a shower, and they went to sleep. After he started snoring, I called my mom, pretending to be frantic. I told her I couldn't take it anymore. I told her that Liam had snatched me up, screamed at me, and threatened me. I wasn't even crying, but I faked my best sobs. I even tried making my voice shake, just for her. I don't know why. I just didn't want to feel like the bad guy anymore. I wanted to feel like I wasn't the problem, and they were.

The next day, my mom had already called Judith and told her about what happened. She even added that Liam had "choked me out." She was desperate to see me, to comfort me. She just wanted to save me. Surprisingly, it wasn't hard for her to picture her son as a monster, even though she raised him and knew better. It was like no matter what she knew to be true, it wasn't. Nothing was true unless I said so in her eyes. If I could get emancipated, I wanted Judith on my side. That way, she may consider letting Mitchell and I come to live with her. I needed to leave my options open. I was too far in and ready to do whatever it took.

I thought that Judith would just let Liam have it. She would put him back in his place, beneath me. To my bewilderment, the exact opposite happened. She had pushed him too far. He was done hearing her overstep her parental boundaries. She didn't live in this house, and he wouldn't sit around and listen to her tell him what was happening under his roof. Chance after chance to be helpful, she had only made things worse. She didn't want to make things better for everyone. She only wanted things to be Ava's way. She favored Ava and she was causing an overbearing amount of problems for everyone else in the family because she refused to believe the truth and only wanted to believe Ava. Before he hung up on his own mother, he reiterated that she was done having alone time, special time for Ava. She could text me, or she could call, but there wouldn't be any more of this, giving into Ava and allowing her to lie about everyone else in the household while creating her own reality to live in.

Judith was desperate. She was showing up at the house to "try to talk some sense" in my dad. He blew her off and said that he had been putting up with this charade for a year…she hadn't made anything better. In fact, she had made it worse. I was worse off now than I ever was regarding my attitude and entitlement. "You need to learn to let her go if you love her." Cliché. She informed my dad that I was leaving when I was sixteen, whether he liked it or not. I hated it when she was giving out spoiler alerts. She actually asked him to let me live with her. She lost it when he firmly told her it was never going to happen. She pleaded that I hated living with him. He countered with, of course, she hates it when she has people like her and my mom filling my head with bullshit all of the time. Then she cracked. "She's going to get emancipated"! While escorting her out of his home, he only shook his head. He told her he wished she would open her eyes to reality and said, "Afraid not, that's not the way it works."

Why would he say that? Luckily, I'm not a cat because I had to know the answer. I reached out to my good friend, Mr. Google. Searching for how do I become emancipated. Just another source of disappointment. Judith made it sound like I just turned 16 and then petitioned the court explaining I wasn't happy with following Liam's rules, and they would just let me be emancipated. Reality check. I had to prove that I was living independently (I don't have a job, a car, or a house). I had to prove I could manage my own affairs. I can't even manage my own laundry. When we went on that vacation to King's Island, the first thing Cara and Dad had to do was take me to the store to buy underwear. I hadn't washed any of my underwear, so I only had the pair I wore down with me.

Shit. Cara still makes dinner for me. I have cups filled with curdled milk on my bedside table. I am not even responsible enough to change out the toilet paper roll. I have to prove I have legitimate means and plans for living arrangements following emancipation. Explaining that my plan is to move into someone else's house and live completely dependent on them, well, and the great state of Indiana, will not amuse the judge. And to top off all the ways I don't meet a single one of these requirements; I have to literally have my dad's consent. I feel like Judith has led me astray. I'd been duped.

The only other way for me to become emancipated is to get pregnant. Here I am, wanting something that is definitely a poor decision given my age, lack of ability to care for even a dog, and no feasible way of living independently. I laugh quietly at the hypocrisy of it all. I mean, I want to leave Liam's house so I don't have to have chores. I don't want to have someone else dictating my entire schedule and life while, at the very same time, thinking I should move out and have a child. Thinking of Cara, I know exactly who would be responsible for doing all the shopping, cleaning, cooking, errand running, and baby-caring tasks. All while having to maintain a job to attempt to sustain myself. Me. I am literally running open arms into the very thing I am running away from. Laughable.

I understand why Liam doesn't want me "hiding" in my room all day and night. It can be a very isolating habit. Sometimes it helps, though. Sometimes, I feel like I am having moments of clarity. When I think of having a baby now, I can envision the way my life will turn out. A double-wide trailer, working part-time at a Citgo, pregnant for the second and third time, praying the state never cuts off my welfare. It's that very vision that makes me question myself. What is my real motivation? No child ever sits in kindergarten and tells the class during circle time they want to be a single mom preying on the working class for a sliver of charity. Then again, who will help watch my kids while I work? If I choose to work, I suppose. Mitchell's jobless pothead mother? Or my mother, who has never been able to raise a single one of her own children appropriately?

My mom always makes it sound like Cara and Liam are the problem. They rub it in our faces about how successful they have become and how much money they make. In reality, they worked from the ground up to get what they had. The American Dream at its finest. They should be proud of accomplishing their goals while raising children to be functional members of society. Not so deep down at all, I don't want to become my mother. Hell, I don't even want to live with her.

I feel immediate regret. I feel genuinely like I could vomit. I feel desperate and hopeless. If prayers are heard, I pray my mother will have a rude awakening in court. I pray that she gets a piece of the disappointment she's been feeding me for the last few years.

***

My dad hasn't even brought up the court date. My mom said she got the letter to confirm the date. It's in just two weeks. I know he got the letter. The court would have sent it out. If my mom had sent it, she would have written the address wrong on purpose. If it weren't for Cara and Dad talking intentionally in private more, Cara tapping diligently away on her computer, and Dad buying Khakis for seemingly no reason at all, you wouldn't have known.

My mom called me more in these two weeks than she did for the last eight years. As a matter of fact, when reading through her petition for determining factors, I came to the quick realization that I have been shackled to someone who couldn't have cared less about me. Reading what she thought was important and imagining what Cara would write for my dad to rebut her claims made me feel…bad. I was washed over with self-pity. I imagine Cara would write with ferocious professionalism and much more detail something like this:

1) Amber had ample opportunities to come to visit with me to help strengthen our bond and build a relationship, and she chose not to...she didn't even have a job. She could have come if she wanted. 2) Amber has never come down for even one day to visit with me. 3) Amber never visited me on my birthday. Not even once in 8 years.

4) Amber fails to take advantage of the parenting time and let me stay with my dad during her scheduled visitation.

5) Amber hasn't shown interest in my health (unless you count her telling my dad to drug test me).

6) Amber hasn't been involved with a single project, homework assignment, or studying with me.

7) Amber never came to a single soccer game, basketball game, or football game (for cheer) to support me...even when I practically begged her to.

8) Amber has lied to me over and over. She breaks every promise she ever made to me.

9) Amber can't take care of herself, let alone me. She depends on the State of Indiana and can't afford me without this assistance.

10) After all the abuse, neglect, and patterns of trauma, I now suffer from anxiety and depression. Amber uses my ultimate

desire (from abandonment wounds) to be wanted by her. She uses this to her advantage and manipulates me.

If dad and Cara told the courts this, it would all be true. The sadness of my story is that she never wanted me. Leftovers. Plain and simple. She only wanted me if there was something in it for her. She couldn't stand the idea of me being happy while she lived eternally lonely and unwanted herself. She couldn't stand the idea of someone else loving and caring for me despite the fact that she wouldn't. She shackled me.

She shackled my heart to the cold, dead remnants within her own chest. She traded my heart for power. She traded my flesh to a monster. She shackled my dreams of being a child to her lonely soul. She traded my safety for desire. She traded my trust for loyalty. She failed to protect me from the horrors of violence that shook my childhood. She shackled my spirit to her bruised body. In the end, through telling this story, I realized she traded my precious but fragile memories for revenge. She shackled my desire for independence to her distorted co-dependency, a trauma bond.

Liam wouldn't discuss court with me. I knew the day had come. Amber told me. She had me up the night before, rehearsing her lines like the actress she was. She had received a letter from the court after her petition. It was my dad's rebuttal. It was very well written. Just as I suspected, Cara had definitely written it for him.

It outlined the harsh truth about Amber she was never a good mother to me. It summarized how little effort she had given in the last 8 years. It portrayed a woman befriending me to salvage a relationship she chose not to have. It perfectly highlighted all the mundane and amazing things Cara and he had done for me over the years. It quite frankly depicted a woman who never met and had no reasonable plan to ever meet the requirements of caring for a child. Amber was particularly pissed about the subtle jabs Cara had placed throughout the list of best interest factors. For example, she mentioned that my dad had a stable home with a very consistent list of household members who were well-bonded. At the same time, pointing out my mother having a laundry list of live-in boyfriends shuffling through her home. Cara so kindly pointed out that all my mother's children had been fathered by different men…and none of them had stuck around. She was an expert in blended families, for sure. She had blended mine with every man in the community.

That morning, Amber had called to remind me she was going to court that day. By the end of the day, we would be well on our way to moving me out of Liam's and into her place. It would probably take a month or so to get the child support order changed and to get the first check, but eventually, with Liam's money, she could start getting herself back on track.

I went to school, but I was filled with dread. She had a list of prepared stories we had walked through together to share with the judge. She had made a false CPS report about a year before. She was planning on bringing it up but would fail to mention that the allegations were found to be untrue. She asked the school counselor to come as a witness (the one I told her I had been working over with lies). She had asked my Grandma Judith to be a witness (they had become pretty good buddies because of me). She was sure, with all of this and a statement of my preference to be living with her, that she would walk out finally triumphant over my father. I was sure that on my 16th birthday, I would wish for a time machine to take back everything that I had done.

Those were my morning worries. By the time school ended, my dad had pulled me aside and said there was something he wanted to talk to me about in private. This was it. The court had concluded, and Amber was getting her wish.

Except it wasn't. The court had concluded. He told me he went to court today. I almost forgot that he hadn't told me about it. He was telling me like it was brand new information. He couldn't be dumb enough to think Amber hadn't told me. He said my mother had filed an emergency petition with the court to be heard about the change in custody…and she had lost. He added that he expected, with this news, that I would accept it. I would be staying with him until I became an adult, and therefore, I needed to start working on getting better. Everyone else in the house was putting in effort, and I needed to start. "We needed to get back to normalcy in the house."

I listened quietly. I didn't say anything. I didn't ask any questions. I didn't want to ruin this moment. Every part of me was grateful to the judge. Just when I thought I was at rock bottom with no way back out of the pit, she had given me a way.

Amber did not take the decision well. She was furious. She called the judge every name she could think of…anything but your honor. She went in and demanded that the judge reschedule the date. Apparently, the school counselor declined to come. She couldn't come at the last minute (I bet she just didn't want to be involved). Judith had a moment of rational thinking and declined to come. She didn't want to be involved with something she had never witnessed and didn't want to inadvertently lie about her own son. She had no witnesses and needed time to coax them into coming after all. The judge declined to reschedule. Apparently, you can't tell the judge there is an emergency and you fear for someone's safety and livelihood and then also ask for a reschedule.

She tried feeding the judge the stories we had come up with together. "Hearsay". She didn't want to hear people's opinions. She very specifically didn't want to hear the opinion of "a child." She said even if my mom's witnesses had been present, she wouldn't have wasted her time hearing them. "Hearsay". She said children have the tendency to lie and exaggerate stories when they want to get out of trouble or want something they can't have.

This isn't the story my mom shared with me. She told me it was all my grandma's fault. If she had come, the judge would have ruled in our favor. She told me my grandma was a bitch and betrayed us. She said the judge took my dad's side because he makes good money. The court only likes rich people. She promised to appeal the decision. I know she is lying. And for once, I am glad she breaks promises.

Later I heard through Judith and by eavesdropping that the judge called my mom out for not being prepared. She called her out for not having any supporting documents. No proof of any of her allegations. No CPS reports. No police report. Nothing. My mom was yelled at for overtalking the judge. She was yelled at for bickering with my dad in the courtroom. My mom threatened to get a lawyer to appeal her decision, and the judge all but laughed in her face and told her she highly encouraged it because she obviously didn't know the law and didn't understand what an emergency petition was for. She said that's why lawyers "get paid the big bucks" because they knew what they were doing, and my mom didn't. She had wasted the courts and my dad's time.

On top of this, she called my Grandma Judith after it was over and threatened her. My mom threatened to not only beat my dad and Cara's ass, but she was going to beat my grandma's ass as well. Overnight, she had trained to be the next ultimate fighter, I guess. Her brother threatened to shoot up my dad's truck at pick-up. Judith told my dad but didn't report the threats to the police. Even now, it was like she didn't want to get on my mom's bad side. My mom said she was never going to speak to Judith again. Probably for the best, really.

Chapter Twenty-Two: Learning to Heal

Forgiveness is a Tricky Concept

Since court, my behaviors have done a quick 180. I immediately stopped throwing temper tantrums. I immediately stopped telling my dad I hated him. My counselor, Brittany laughed that she didn't even recognize me as the same teen she had been seeing. Not only had I stopped my piss-poor behaviors, but I started telling my dad I loved him at night. I started coming downstairs. I started going out with the family without causing a scene. It was like something out of a fairytale. I was cursed, and the judge's ruling had broken the spell.

Wouldn't it be nice if it actually worked that way in real life? It took my mom two years to brainwash me into thinking things were wrong at my dad's house. I couldn't possibly reverse everything I had worked to destroy in that first week after court. I wanted to try to mend some relationships. Brittany seems to think that I might be a common denominator in my problems.

I could be friends and enjoy Ella again. I was slowly reaching out to her. I started inviting her to play video games with me. I started confiding in her. I invited myself into her room. I talked about the problems I was having with Mitchell. He was being selfish and wanted to hang out online with his friends, not with me. I told her I was going to gaslight him into feeling guilty for not spending his every waking second with me. She said, "That's toxic and not a healthy part of a relationship." I left the room I invited myself into.

I am still jealous of her. I still want to pick on her and belittle her. I still want to call her names, call her fat. I still want her to feel inferior to me. I do try to bite my tongue sometimes, but I'm not good at it. I didn't use a filter for two years. I am learning that I shouldn't treat her this way. I am learning that if I learn to heal from my hurt, I won't want her to hurt like me. It's part of my trauma response.

I attempted to reach out to Layla. I sent her a sincere apology. Well, as sincere as I am capable of being in this chapter of my life. She didn't respond. She's not as easy to manipulate into forgiving me. That hurts me. I am jealous that she has been missing Ella and sending her messages. She doesn't miss me, and that silence is overwhelmingly loud, deafening. I need to move forward and let her go to heal, but it's so much harder to do than it sounds in therapy. It's hard to reflect on things that have made me happy without thinking about her.

As I mentioned, not everything is better. There is still an awkwardness in the house. People don't know how to act when I come around. They are still unsure of which Ava they are going to have an interaction with that day. My dad is working with me. Cara is still trucking along, doing all her motherly things.

Somedays, I still want to fight. I revert to my old, self-entitled, emotionally dysregulated self. I still try to pick fights with my dad. I still tell him he's the problem in my life. I tried to convince him that he was an absent father and never had time for me. I try to convince him that he loves Ella more than me. I accuse him of not giving me the attention that I need. I still look for someone to blame. It's hard for me to take accountability for my own behaviors. Our fights don't get as loud, and they don't last as long. I'm sure he considers that progress a win for him.

It's easier to be fooled than it is to admit that you have been fooled. My mom never filed that appeal. I think she can see that I am a handful. If Cara is right, she made me this way, but now she doesn't want to deal with the monster she created.

Steve left her. He told me if I wasn't going to be living with him, he didn't want to stay with her (read whatever you want into that). My mom says she caught him cheating on her. If he's smart, he'll follow through with his plan and he will petition the court for custody of my youngest brother. He'll probably win. She'll be desperate to find another man soon enough, and I will be packed right back into that Tupperware bowl.

Cara and Dad threw me a party for my sixteenth birthday. I

wasn't getting a car like most teens do on their sixteenth birthday. I was lucky to have the party, I guess. I acted like I didn't want the party. I acted like I didn't want the decorations that Cara ordered. She worked all week but still planned the party. She still ordered the decorations and the cake. She was so excited to reveal the festive balloons. She threw me a taco bar party. She made beef and chicken tacos. She made burritos and nachos. She got me a taco-shaped cake. She made me a banner that said, "Taco bout a sweet 16". She threw me a party I didn't deserve. I didn't get a car, but they did buy me some really nice Airpods.

They made me feel special. They made me feel like a wanted part of this family, even after I made them feel like shit. I know Cara confided to her best friend over the years all of the terrible things I put her through, but even her best friend came on my birthday. This was a good day. On good days, I want to heal. I want to let go of my hate and hurt.

My dad has been good about driving me around town to go on dates with Mitchell. They have even let him come over to our house a few times, supervised of course. It's hard to explain why they "were such terrible tyrants" just a few months ago but were suddenly these understanding and accommodating parents now. They hang out downstairs while we watch movies or carve pumpkins.

Despite the good, I still accuse my dad of not giving enough. I begged him just to let Mitchell and I go in the basement alone. I tell him we aren't going to have sex if that's what he's worried about. I tell him Mitchell won't even kiss me when he is around. I just want to feel alone with Mitchell. I want to explore him and give him intimate attention. I want to express my love for him in the ways adults do, without my dad and Cara watching us on the couch upstairs. He didn't budge. It wasn't going to happen. Normally, I would lash out at him and tell him how much I despised him and hated him. I would have gone days without speaking to him, but now, because I am trying, I say a few choice words, but I drop it.

At one point, Cara had told me that I needed to take everything I could from counseling. Not for her sake, to improve our relationship, even though that would be a bonus, but to help learn how to develop healthier coping strategies. She thinks that if I don't learn how to communicate better, build my self-esteem, and work on my trust and abandonment issues, I will end up sabotaging all my relationships, both friendships and intimate relationships.

Right now, I am living to be Mitchell's girlfriend, hoping to be his future wife. I stalk his location with my phone. I get upset when I can't talk to him, and at times, pretend to be feeling ill just so I can stay home, waiting for his call. Cara says there is a difference between love and obsession. She asked me what was different about the way I felt about Daniel and how I felt about

Mitchell. I tell her I was obsessed with Daniel, but I am in love with Mitchell. If that is true, she wonders why I am treating them the same and following the same patterns of behavior. She may be right. I accuse Mitchell of not showing me he loves me (even though he got me a promise ring and tattooed my name on his collarbone). I tell him I have all these feelings and he must not have any because he never shows me. He's cold and heartless. I guilt him into giving me attention and, yes, even money to show he loves me.

I recently got a job…you guessed it at Perkins. There was a hostess position open. I couldn't resist working there with Mitchell. I'm hoping there is a lot of downtime so I can head into the kitchen and the back area just to be with him. He was able to pull some strings to get me the job. Now, I can make sure he's not on his phone chatting with other girls while he's at work. After work, while Cara waits in the parking lot for me to come out, we sneak outback by the dumpster and kiss good night. This is as close as I can get to him for now.

I want to get back on track. I want to be more focused on my future. I still want to be emancipated and live like I am 25 rather than 16. I still have sporadic moments where I feel the overwhelming urge to beg to have this Nexplanon out of my arm so I can trick Mitchell into getting me pregnant now. I've tried it all. I pretended to bleed for weeks without end when I wasn't really bleeding. I pretend it's causing me cramps rather than my constipation. Those excuses were a dead end. I even tried telling him it was causing me severe weight gain. He told me my insatiable appetite for junk food and fast food was causing the weight gain, not the implant. I guess it'll stay in for now.

When I visit with my mom, she tells me my dad is shit. She hasn't changed. She's still just as negative as before. Her bitterness is contagious. When I spend the weekend with her, I start reverting to my old thoughts. I typically come home with a shitty attitude for the first few days. It's like medicine that has to get through my system for me to get better. Dad is going to let me start driver's training again. I have to be honest; I am looking forward to not going to her house. I'm glad that I "need" to stay at my dad's house for the class. She makes me feel like the person I don't want to be anymore.

I am putting in the effort that Liam asked for. All my life, he gave me everything he possibly could, trying to give me the best life possible. It wouldn't be right for me not to try to give him basic human decency and the respect he deserves.

I'm not good with words like Cara. I'm definitely not good with apologies. But I figured I would give it a shot. I would tell this story and try to ditch pity once and for all. Just once, I decided to write Cara back. Really, I am writing it to everyone I hurt along the way.

Leftovers

This isn't easy for me. I'm not good at admitting when I am wrong. As a matter of fact, I have been actively avoiding it for longer than I can remember. There have been moments I haven't been proud of, moments I have been outright ashamed of. I intentionally ruined things. I tainted everything I touched. I said the worst possible things to people who loved me, trusted me, and should have looked up to me. I burned bridge after bridge. I chose to do the wrong thing on purpose. I chose to idolize someone who treated me like leftovers. I chose not to believe anyone who tried to steer me in the right direction. I chose to give everything up for someone who broke not only promises but also my heart. I know that I can be better. I want to be better. To Zack, I'm sorry I was mischievous and never got to know you better when I had the chance. To Ella, I am truly sorry. You deserved a better sister than the one you got. To Cara, I am sorry I didn't want to love you out loud when you deserved it. To Dad, I am sorry that you whisked me away to a magical place, far away from all the terrible and traumatic things I learned too soon, and I never said thank you. I never showed you the appreciation and respect you deserved. To everyone else, I am sorry I caused the collateral damage without even a moment's hesitation on my self-destructive path.

I know I've been loud and terrible. I have been deceitful and nasty. I've been spiteful and venomous...But PLEASE.

If there is even a scrap of love left in you for me...

PLEASE don't give up on me now.

-Ava

About the Author

Nikki Adkins is a new author who juggles a full-time job in the medical field with her passion for writing. When she is not caring for patients, she finds solace in writing captivating fiction stories. As a married mother of three children, Nikki understands the importance of finding time for herself, and writing serves as her ultimate stress reliever. In addition to writing, she loves to read and be outdoors.

9 798330 305957